DOCTOR WHO

The Forgotten Army

The DOCTOR WHO series from BBC Books

DOCTOR WHO

The Forgotten Army

BRIAN MINCHIN

BBC
BOOKS

1 3 5 7 9 10 8 6 4 2

Published in 2011 by BBC Books, an imprint of Ebury Publishing.
A Random House Group Company

Doctor Who is a BBC Wales production for BBC One.
Executive producers: Steven Moffat, Piers Wenger and Beth Willis

The Random House Group Limited Reg. No. 954009

Addresses for companies within the Random House Group can be found at
www.randomhouse.co.uk

A CIP catalogue record for this book is available from the British Library.

ISBN 9781849903134

The Random House Group Limited supports The Forest Stewardship Council
(FSC®), the leading international forest certification organisation. Our books
carrying the FSC label are printed on FSC® certified paper. FSC is the only forest
certification scheme endorsed by the leading environmental organisations,
including Greenpeace. Our paper procurement policy can be found at
www.randomhouse.co.uk/environment

Commissioning editor: Albert DePetrillo
Series consultant: Justin Richards
Project editor: Steve Tribe
Cover design: Lee Binding © Woodlands Books Ltd, 2010
Production: Rebecca Jones

Printed and bound in Great Britain by
CPI Group (UK) Ltd, Croydon, CR0 4YY

To buy books by your favourite authors and register for offers,
visit www.randomhouse.co.uk

To Robert

Sam Horwitz had never felt so excited. The Grand Hall of the New York Natural History Museum was packed with hundreds of people, all clutching invitations to 'See the New Wonder of the World'. In exactly two minutes, Sam was going to step out and show them his amazing discovery.

Sam fidgeted with his new white blazer. He'd never worn anything so bold before, but for this, the biggest day of his life, he wanted to impress. He had worked alone throughout the night to get the mysterious exhibit ready, and only he and the Director of the Museum knew what was hidden behind the thick velvet drapes.

Looking around the room, he felt dizzy with adrenalin. There were massed rows of schoolchildren and their grumpy teachers, bearded archaeologists, twitchy photographers, and the great and good of New York. He saw his friend Polly Vernon give him a little wave from the middle of the crowd. Polly was a teacher at a New York elementary school and had brought all of her class to cheer him on. He smiled nervously as she mouthed an encouraging 'good luck'. At the front, jostling for position, all the major TV stations were preparing to broadcast the first pictures live to the world. Sam knew they weren't going to be disappointed.

The Director of the Museum finished her introduction and called on Sam to take the stand. Sam took a deep breath. Everything was about to change. He was about to become famous.

He strode across the Grand Hall to loud applause and stood blinking as camera lights flashed. The news crews signalled to each other: they were going live. Sam knew this was his big moment. All around the world, millions of people would be watching. Sam felt happier than he'd ever been. Those long weeks digging in the icy wastes of Svalbard had been worth it.

Sam stepped up to the podium, trying hard not to fiddle with his jacket buttons. He'd rehearsed this moment over and over again: a short thank you, a joke to show to everyone he was a down-to-earth kind of guy, then he'd pull the cord and bask in their applause.

He reached the microphone, shuffled his papers and began to speak. 'Thank you, everyone, for coming. Today our ideas of the past are about to change for ever. We've had plenty of big displays in this Museum, but I can promise you, this is our most mammoth yet!'

Sam pulled the golden cord, and the velvet drapes dropped aside to reveal the world's only Polar Woolly Mammoth. It was one of the most majestic creatures ever to grace the Grand Hall. Standing four metres tall, the mammoth looked wild, with rippling white fur and long tusks. Yet it was also strangely graceful, like a thoroughbred horse, ready to spring from the traps.

Sam knew that no one could fail to be impressed by its grandeur and size. It was as if the forces of evolution had sought to create in the Polar Woolly Mammoth the largest and most beautiful creature ever. But there were no gasps of awe – the crowd had fallen silent. They were stunned and shocked, not delighted. Something was wrong. Sam started to feel sick in his stomach, like the day before a big exam. He turned to follow the anxious gaze of his audience.

The Polar Woolly Mammoth had been extinct for 10,000 years, and the body of this one had been lying under the ice cap for almost all that time. It now stood at the centre of the New York Natural History Museum, in a beautiful recreation of its original habitat. So Sam was as surprised as everyone else to see four fresh mammoth poos splatting onto the floor.

Plop. Plop. Plop. Plop.

One of the schoolchildren started to giggle, and a wave of laughter spread across the hall. Polly's class of kids were clapping with delight, loving the joke that they thought was being played on them.

The Director of the Museum turned to Sam with a face like thunder. 'Is this your idea of a practical joke?'

'N-no!' Sam stuttered. He was as surprised as everyone else. The mammoth was dead. He'd found it buried under a hundred metres of solid ice. It was so dead no one could even remember a time it had existed.

Then the mammoth let out an enormous roar, and the hall erupted into chaos and screams and scuffling feet. The largest mammoth ever discovered had come back to life. All around the Grand Hall, people were leaping from their seats and running to the back of the hall. The giggles had turned into tears. This was very real, very scary and very wrong. Sam could see the news crews broadcasting the pandemonium, jabbering excitedly as the cameras swung between the slowly waking mammoth and the stampede of people in the hall behind them.

Sam started to speak into the microphone. 'Please stay calm. This, er, isn't unusual – this room is very hot, and the mammoth has been frozen for quite some time… We can put this down to environmental factors… gas being released… er… It's nothing to worry about at all…'

Nobody was listening. As the world watched live on television, the only known Polar Woolly Mammoth ripped its feet from the podium. Very much alive, and very annoyed at being tied down.

Clearly panicking that it was going to break out and run riot on the streets of New York, the Director of the Museum yelled, 'Close the doors!' Black-clad security guards slammed the heavy wooden doors of the New York Museum shut, large iron bolts barring the only way out of the building.

Stepping closer to Sam, the Director of the Museum whispered furiously in his ear: 'Find a way to stop this. And do it now!' She marched away.

Polly appeared at Sam's side and fixed him with big trusting eyes. 'What should I do?'

Sam couldn't bear the look on her face. He had asked her to bring her students here, and now he'd let loose a prehistoric animal on them.

Behind him, the mammoth was stretching its enormous jaws, its long tusks scraping the floor of the Museum. It had been asleep for a long, long time. And now it was awake, and it was very, very angry. Its plate-sized eyes fixed on Sam, and it started to advance towards him.

Sam wanted desperately to stay calm. He wished

he could find something reassuring to say. Instead, as the mammoth's heavy feet began to pound on the wooden floor, he turned to Polly and yelled, 'Run! Whatever it takes, get everyone out of here!'

Chapter
1

'**New York, New York!** Or is it New, New, New, New, New, New, New York?' The Doctor was turning in circles, rattling off words at a bewildering speed.

Amy looked at the Doctor as if he was mad. 'Hey, elbow-patches – look at the clock!'

Sure enough, right above them in Times Square, the date was beaming down for all to see.

The Doctor smiled. 'I got it right this time! Finally – 2010. Have I impressed you yet?'

Amy reckoned she had a pretty good line in rash and unpremeditated, but she'd found a real rival in the Doctor. She wasn't about to let him know it, though. 'Why New York? I thought we were going to the Moons of Poosh, or the Sapphire Beaches of Padparashan 2? I'm not missing *X-Factor* so much I need to stop by in 2010 and play catch-up.'

'Look around you, Amy. Isn't it glorious? Just smell the air! On second thoughts, forget the air, just look up.'

Above them, skyscrapers of all sorts and shapes thrust up into the sky, as if the city had been in far too much of a hurry to plan what it was doing. It had wanted to reach the top, and had done anything to get there.

The sun was almost blotted out by the buildings all around them, and it felt to Amy as if they were walking in a deep valley, thronging with noisy, busy, excited, people. Everywhere she looked was a blaze of colour: yellow cabs beeping angrily, tourists posing for pictures, and lights blazing out of every display. Amy had never seen so many people in one place, or so much going on at one time. She was a long way from Leadworth and Mrs Poggitt whinging about her bad hip.

New York was all Amy had imagined and more. But Amy was used to getting people to do exactly what she wanted, whenever she wanted, and she didn't want the Doctor to think he could get away with bossing her around all over the universe, and springing surprises on her, even if they were nice ones. Part of Amy loved that the Doctor was a law unto himself. But the other part of Amy Pond saw a challenge. She knew he was harder to twist around her fingers than the other men in her life, but she wasn't about to give in to his bossiness just yet.

'So gimme, psychic paper, over here,' she told him. 'Two hours is all I need. I'm going to find out how much shopping we can fit into that TARDIS of yours.'

The Doctor moved in front of the police box doors, as if he was protecting them from her. 'I show you the wonders of time and space, and you want to buy them?' he asked, appalled.

Amy laughed. 'As if I'd be so boring! Whatever you want to do, for say, ten minutes, then my turn? Sound good to you?'

The Doctor didn't answer. His attention had been grabbed by the sights and sounds of Times Square.

Amy tried again to break in on his thoughts. 'So what have you got for me this time? Do you need us to sort out some Mafia deal? Problems with a gang of cowboys? Or a Wall Street billionaire that's really an alien? Actually, forget the others – let's focus on the Wall Street billionaire.'

The Doctor's thoughts were racing ahead. 'New York. It's the sort of place that things happen, always worth checking up on New York, make sure no one's flying around in gravity bubbles a few years early. I like to keep track of it, especially now I'm looking all fresh and new. And don't look at my bow tie like that, Pond. Bow ties are cool. Anyway, always good to make sure there's no cracks in it.'

While Amy tried to work out if it was cracks

in New York or cracks in his bow ties that were worrying him, the Doctor flicked his gaze from the city to his sonic screwdriver, which was flashing a light he'd never seen before. Excited, he turned his attention to Amy. 'Just look at that! Now, this is very important. There's a museum in the 175th century I need to show you, but the canteen is rubbish: they only eat boiled Jericoacoara beans. Don't ask me why; it's a religious thing. Anyway, you deserve the best the universe has to offer – and it's here!'

He held his sonic screwdriver up to Amy, so she could see the row of flashing lights.

'Do I look like a dolphin?' Amy demanded. 'What does that mean for those of us that can't decipher sonic technology?'

The Doctor grinned. 'It means I was right!' He spun on the spot, scanning Times Square with the sonic screwdriver. 'There's a place I've always wanted to go, dreamed of it, hoped for it, but I've been constantly disappointed, always losing track. I've leapt through constellations and danced around black holes just to get the name of this place. And it's been here all along! Don't you just love New York? You never know what you're going to find!'

Amy held up her hand. 'Whoa there! What are you talking about?'

'I've just picked up a very special signal,' the Doctor explained. He twirled his sonic screwdriver in his hand. 'And what it confirms is that there's a restaurant here that will one day be the most famous in all of the galaxy. In the 208th century, people are so obsessed with it they travel back through time from all over the galaxy to eat there. Well, I say people... *Anything* with less than four stomachs travels to eat here at least once a lifetime. It's renowned as the best meal you will ever have. Will have had. Had ever having. Sorry, time travel tenses, they're very confusing. Just stick with me. This is the most famous food in the galaxy and people spend a lifetime of savings to make the trip. And we've landed in the perfect vintage. The Ood Food Guide gave June 2010 a whole solar system of awards. Good old TARDIS!'

The Doctor patted the side of the police box and clicked his fingers. With barely a whirr, the TARDIS faded from sight.

The Doctor saw Amy's expression and quickly reassured her. 'I've just left it a few seconds ahead of us. I'll get it back when it's time to leave. No point confusing people.'

Amy couldn't help but be caught up in the Doctor's enthusiasm. 'So is this what we do then? Sometimes we save the world; other times we're like space tourists.'

'Yep. But we're the best sort. We don't, you know, stay up all night and go starting fights. Actually, who am I kidding, we're the worst sort...' Marching off, the Doctor led Amy into a busy side street. 'And just look at the queue. Barely a human amongst them.'

Sure enough, the anonymous alley was packed with very strangely shaped people.

'Are they really aliens? In the middle of New York?' Amy asked. 'They just look sort of… *American* to me.'

The Doctor nodded. 'It's not a problem, they're very well behaved. Not like the French. Look, no pushing at all.' As they walked along the queue, he started pointing out individuals. 'Now, the one in the trench coat is a Judoon. The one that looks like three people standing on top of each other is a Graske. The girl in the shades and the hairy chin? Cat person! Very naughty coming here, but, hey – when the food is this good, you can't blame her, can you?'

Amy joined in. 'My turn! Look, that hideous man there, kind of horrible droopy face and weirdy eyes, that's got to be something – maybe a mutant from Mars. Or you know, a giant space slug or something?'

'Shh!' The Doctor leaned in close to Amy. 'That's Kenny, nice guy, works in the Post Office. Don't worry, I'm sure he gets compared to aliens all the time!'

They followed the queue down the alley and turned into a big open courtyard. The Doctor stopped. 'Smell that, Amy!'

The food smelt like crisp onions, frying chips

and sizzling meat.

'This is the holy grail of food! I never quite thought it would happen, but now here we are!'

As the assorted people stood aside, Amy could see where they were heading. She was expecting to see something like the Ritz, all marble and glitz. Instead, the Doctor was heading for a battered old trolley, where a weary-looking man was flipping burgers behind a row of brightly coloured sauces. Pinned behind him was a giant sign: 'Big Paulie's Sausages'.

Amy was confused. 'Why's it say sausages? He's selling burgers!'

The Doctor was too excited to answer. 'Oh, isn't this just brilliant! Look at everyone here! All so happy.'

He pointed at a large table of what looked like seagulls in duffel coats. 'Where they come from, they've been at war for five hundred years, but they're barely waving a fork at each other here. If one thing is going to save the universe, it's one of Big Paulie's Sausage-Burgers.'

Sitting on tables laid out on the sidewalk, the disguised aliens sighed with pleasure as they tasted the famous burgers. At one table, a family of Haemo-Goths spat into the air as a sign of their appreciation, long tongues flickering in and out.

'They have a restaurant in the Luxury Zone of the Ruby Solar System where they cook everything in liquid nitrogen. When you put it in your mouth it foams right up inside your nose. Smells delicious. Tastes a bit like bogies. But never mind that. This is all about The Burgers! Do you ever get that feeling where you'd do anything for a burger? And right here, right now is the very best place in history to get a burger. Of course there's a twelve-year waiting list, just to eat one. But *I* have come prepared.'

Amy looked at the Doctor, unimpressed. 'You rang ahead?'

The Doctor shook his head. 'Nope. You'll like this. I've bought the street. In your name! As the owner, you get free burgers for life. I recommend the Doctor Burger. It's like a cheeseburger but with extra bacon, sausage and steak. And a bit of chicken, I think. No ketchup though. Absolutely banned. Yucky stuff.'

Amy thought this was a good time to assert herself. 'OK, Doctor. But after this, we go shopping, yeah? No running off, no flirting with 500-year-olds.'

'I was just being friendly!'

'And this time, if we find a hot man in uniform, he's coming with us. That's not a problem, is it?'

Straightening his bow tie, the Doctor turned to Amy and opened his mouth to reply. Then something grabbed his attention. 'Oooh, that's interesting…' He gazed over Amy's shoulder into the distance.

Amy waved a hand in front of his face. 'Hey!

Don't drift off, just when you're about to agree with me!'

The Doctor was suddenly serious. 'Amy, everyone in Times Square has just stopped. Do you know how often that happens? That *never* happens…'

Looking around them, Amy could see the humans in the queue answering their phones, and all turning to look up the alley.

The Doctor grabbed Amy's hand and ran back up the alleyway into an almost silent Times Square.

'I bet you weren't so grumpy when you were here before.' A thought crossed Amy's mind. 'Did you come here with another girl?'

The Doctor smiled. 'Don't look at me like that, Pond. You've been on other dates; I've been to other New Yorks. And this isn't a date, before you ask, and neither was the other time, sorry, times, and I choose to look at it, at like – Oooh! What *is* happening up there?'

On the massive digital screen above them, a headline scrolled in bold red capitals: CHAOS AT THE MUSEUM. On every screen in Times Square, the same three-second burst of action was playing over and over again: a frenzied white mammoth leaping off a stand, turning its head and roaring at a terrified and cowering man in a bright white jacket.

All around them, people were staring open-mouthed at the screens.

The Doctor was smiling, struggling to hide his

excitement. 'Now that is more like it! The burgers can wait!'

'That poor man!' Amy cried. 'Look how scared he looks.'

Up on the screens, live CCTV camera footage showed that the Museum had emptied of people, but one man remained. It was the man in the distinctive white blazer, and he was vainly trying to hook a velvet rope around the mammoth's leg.

'That's either very brave or very stupid,' the Doctor remarked. 'And it'll never work. We'd better get a move on.' He took Amy's hand and led her across the road.

'How do you know the way?' Amy asked as they started to run up Broadway.

'In an emergency, always head for the helicopters...' the Doctor told her with a smile.

Sure enough, several helicopters were passing overhead, news crews and armed police all heading for the New York Natural History Museum.

The Doctor gazed up at them. 'Think we can thumb a lift?'

Amy shot her arm out in front of a yellow cab and yelled, 'TAXI!'

The car screeched to a halt, and Amy opened the door. 'Thank you. Very important business. My man has my credentials.'

The Doctor stood dumbstruck.

'Come on, dumbo.' Amy waggled her fingers.

'The papers…'

The Doctor twigged, and passed her the psychic paper. She waved it at the driver, who jumped out of his car, saluted clumsily, and held the door as Amy got in.

'I've always wanted to do that,' Amy murmured happily as the Doctor clambered in beside her. 'Looks pretty happy to be helping the Empress of Scotland, doesn't he.'

'What does that make me?' the Doctor asked.

Amy smiled. 'You're my bag carrier, of course.'

Sam's day was still going very, very badly. After the screaming crowds had fled, he had stayed behind just long enough for the heavy doors to be sealed again. Now he was alone with a prehistoric animal, and he was feeling very scared. He had hidden himself in the cloakroom, and was peering out from behind a row of Puffa jackets, watching the mammoth pacing the Museum's Grand Hall.

As it moved in slow circles around the room, the mammoth growled in frustration at each locked door. It was looking for a way out, Sam realised, wondering what it would do if it stayed trapped for much longer. Frustrated by its captivity, the creature had already smashed the reception desk with a casual flick of its leg, and then set about destroying the priceless Barosaurus skeleton with sharp stabs of its tusks.

Sam felt responsible. He had spent months of his life tending to the mammoth, and he knew every inch of its furry body. He was aware of an unnerving instinct telling him this was a faithful pet that would recognise him and do as he said. But the more the mammoth roared and stamped on its surroundings, the less Sam believed he could have an influence on the savage beast.

Nothing he had learnt about biology had prepared him for this. Sam couldn't get over how impossible it all was. The mammoth had been frozen for thousands and thousands of years. There was no way it could have come back to life.

He tried telling himself that the mammoth was probably as scared of him as he was of it, and that it didn't want to harm anyone... All he had to do was give it what it wanted, and it would calm down. But a sinking feeling told him that what the mammoth wanted was feeding, and at the moment Sam was the only food in the room.

There was something else, too – some nagging detail. Sam was sure that when the creature had first roared, he'd heard a strange high-pitched noise, like the precise clicking of a thousand tiny cogs. He was the only person close enough to hear it but, to Sam, it had almost seemed as if someone, somewhere was laughing...

Chapter
2

As their cab zoomed past Central Park, Amy quizzed the Doctor. 'What's the diagnosis, then? Is this an alien cloaking itself as a mammoth to hide its true evil features? Or maybe some evil life force has possessed an innocent mammoth and brought it back to life?'

The Doctor looked stern. 'If we're lucky...'

'What does that mean?' Amy asked. 'If we're lucky...'

The Doctor didn't answer. Something was clearly troubling him.

Amy pressed him harder. 'We're here to protect it, right? Stop any trigger-happy cop killing the poor thing.' She punched the Doctor lightly on the arm. 'Oi! I'm talking to you here!'

The Doctor turned to Amy. 'I've travelled light years to see new species before, and there's something wrong with this… Why is this white mammoth even alive? I mean, whoever heard of a *white* mammoth, anyway? And why is it here now?'

They reached the corner of Central Park West and 79th Street and leapt out into a scrum of gawpers and onlookers.

As he pulled away, the cab driver yelled, 'I'm honoured, your Majesty,' and Amy gave a regal wave of her hand.

In front of the Doctor and Amy, heavily armed police were gathering around a mobile command centre, while NYPD cops put up barriers in front of the Museum entrance.

Amy paused to survey the crowd in front of them, but the Doctor headed straight off into the crowds. Amy caught up with him as he arrived at the police barrier and, with a huge grin on his face, introduced himself.

'Hello, I'm the Doctor. I hear you've got a bit of pest problem… Papers, Pond, papers.'

Amy flashed the Doctor's psychic paper, and the police officer saluted. 'Good to see you, sir! Been a while since we needed the Official City Animal Wrangler. Didn't actually know we still had one.'

The Doctor smiled. 'Protecting the city with a smile since 1861. Now, at ease, can we get all these barriers taken down, please? A bit of space for my work and I'll have this under control in no time.' He nodded at Amy. 'Along with my friend, the Assistant Official City Animal Wrangler.'

The officer looked troubled. 'There's been orders from the top, sir. No way can we interfere with their jurisdiction.' He leant in close to the Doctor and whispered. 'The Men in Black are on their way. Commander Strebbins has taken charge until they get here.'

Amy turned to where the officer was pointing, and saw a serious-looking woman in an all-black suit pacing purposefully near a mobile base of operations. She was giving stern orders to a young officer, who relayed them into his walkie-talkie. The woman seemed to reach a decision, gesturing with a raised hand. As one, the armed police marksmen fanned out across the entrance and took up position, aiming their guns at the Museum door.

The Doctor was not happy. 'No, no, no, no, this is all wrong…'

Next to Amy, a news reporter started speaking direct to camera. Amy could make out the words 'armed response unit… compassionate killing… minimise risk to civilians…'

'Trinity Wells will be here soon,' the Doctor suddenly announced, and Amy watched a big grin light up his face.

'She one of your old flames?' she asked, intrigued.

The Doctor smiled. 'Never met her, actually.'

On cue, the AMN news helicopter appeared overhead as the Doctor continued. 'The thing is, people think I'm bad news, but every time I see Trinity on the telly, I know the world's in terrible danger.'

More armoured vans pulled up in front of the Museum, and heavily protected police came piling out, bulky with bulletproof suits and helmets. Commander Strebbins waved them into position and, to her horror, Amy saw an officer pull a bazooka out of a case. Amy was sure she caught the command 'lock and load'.

The Doctor took Amy's mobile out of her pocket and zapped it with his sonic screwdriver. There was a burst of static and they instantly heard the police radio signals.

'–o Nine, in position – I have eyeball on the west door – awaiting orders – confirm live ammunition – no casualties recorded – tear gas on standby – will enter on confirmation of news media blackout – Zero Nine, over and out.'

Around them, the crowd had grown quieter in expectation of an unhappy ending. The onlookers could sense this was going to be brutal. Amy was sure she could hear a child crying somewhere nearby. She felt as glum as the Doctor. Something as incredible as a mammoth had come to New York, and the police were preparing to kill it. She couldn't believe how people could become so cruel just because they'd met something they were scared of.

Amy turned to the Doctor, upset. 'This is terrible, Doctor. What are we going to do?'

The Doctor looked worried. 'We can't let it be killed, who knows what will happen... Maybe I could use what they have to help... The thing is, Amy, we need to get to it before anyone does anything stupid... Amy? Amy!'

But Amy wasn't waiting. It was time for action. She walked straight up to the mobile command centre and accosted the nearest police officer, practically grabbing him by his lapels. By the time the Doctor caught up, she was in full flow: 'Right then, Detective Pond here, courtesy of the TARDIS Division of New Scotland Yard, Scottish branch.... You've been told we were coming. No?'

The cop was shaking his head. Amy stepped even closer to him, standing at her full height.

'What's your name?' she demanded.

'Officer Henderson.'

'First name?'

'Oscar,' the young officer replied, surprised.

'Right then, Oscar, I'm Amy. I just wanted to ask, has the creature inside killed anyone?'

Oscar seemed to relax slightly. 'No, ma'am, and if you could step back I'd be much obliged. This is a controlled situation.'

Amy wasn't backing down. 'Has it harmed

anyone in any way?'

Again, Oscar shook his head. 'No. But we believe that we should take preventative measures against any threat.'

Amy leant forward, bringing her mouth right up to his ear. Then she yelled, 'SO WHY ARE YOU GOING TO KILL IT?'

Oscar stumbled back, stunned by her ferocity.

The Doctor sprang to the rescue. 'If I can just borrow my friend back, thank you...' As they walked away, he whispered, 'I think there might be an easier way of doing this. Can I borrow your phone again?'

The Doctor rubbed Amy's phone up and down on his jacket like it was a cricket ball and hit it a few times with his sonic screwdriver. 'This should work,' he mumbled and pressed 'Call'.

Moments later, the Doctor was speaking with quiet authority, the big grin back on his face. 'Commander Strebbins, would you know what I meant if I gave you a code X231 hyphen 19 ten?'

There was a momentary silence, punctuated with urgent bursts of static and whispered conversation. Amy glanced over towards Strebbins, who was obviously confused that anyone could radio straight to her. The Doctor seemed to have turned the phone into a police walkie-talkie.

'Let me guess what you're saying.' Amy's attention snapped back to the Doctor, who'd obviously lost patience waiting for Strebbins's answer. 'There'll be no record of the mission allowed, no one in the NYPD or the FBI will be accountable, and you'll have to put your guns downs. No one's going to like it, but you're gonna do it. The short version is: I'm the Doctor – lemme in!' He grinned as he handed the phone back to Amy. 'I love a good code X231 hyphen 19 ten!'

Amy could see the furious Commander Strebbins approaching them. She looked to be in her fifties, and was probably hardened by numerous hours on the street. She was also obviously not used to being told what she could and couldn't do.

The Doctor turned to greet her. 'Hello, I'm the Doctor. You might have heard about me?'

'Colonel Mace was vague on that matter,' Strebbins growled. 'But he seemed to think I'd have no problem letting you take command of this scene. Told me you were worth ten thousand of my men.'

'Old friend,' the Doctor murmured to Amy. 'Always nice to have someone put in a word…'

Commander Strebbins evidently didn't like being kept waiting. She broke in brusquely: 'I'm trained for this situation, Doctor, and we need to go in with maximum force. I have the capacity to take out a creature twenty times the size of that beast. I've got smoke grenades, stun guns, smart explosives, and enough firepower to reduce however many elephants you've got in there to cat food.' She smiled, obviously assuming the matter was closed.

Commander Strebbins had underestimated the Doctor.

'Ah, well that's where there's a problem. Because, no one is going to hurt that creature while I'm here.'

'Damn it, there are people in there, Doctor!' Strebbins more or less shouted. 'I will protect them, whatever the cost.'

'Like shouting at him will make him change his mind,' Amy thought wryly, as the Doctor pulled a tiny pair of binoculars out of his pocket and started gazing towards the Grand Hall of the Museum.

'There's no one in the windows,' he told them, 'which means everyone got out of the place before the mammoth woke up properly. If I'm right, you'll have sealed the doors of the Grand Hall, so it's not going to have gone far. Pretty grand doors in there, if I remember.'

Strebbins gaped, but the Doctor hadn't finished.

'And you're forgetting just how clever and brilliant those people in there are. If they're as good as I think, they'll have run to the top floor, only sensible thing to do when a prehistoric animal comes back to life...' His binoculars shifted up, where he saw a group of schoolchildren waving. 'There they are! Safe on the top floor, probably looking at the crustacean exhibit, lovely seahorses... So, Commander, you were saying?'

Commander Strebbins stared back at the Doctor for several seconds. 'I'll give you thirty minutes. If you get in trouble in there, you're on your own.'

Three minutes later, the Doctor was ready to enter the Museum. Strebbins had reluctantly ordered her marksmen to crawl back from the steps, the armoured trucks had been withdrawn, and the Doctor had given out instructions on how to safely trap a mammoth. Under his keen eye, officers were busily scattering hay over a flatbed truck, and loading up tranquilliser darts.

'This is only a precaution,' the Doctor told them cheerfully. 'We'll lead it out. Probably. My friend here is an expert on wild animals.'

The Doctor nodded at Amy. From the way the police officers looked her up and down, Amy guessed she wasn't their idea of a zoologist. She nodded back, trying to radiate a convincing air of professional beast-tamer.

The Doctor turned back to the men and told them exactly when they should open the doors, and what to have ready for when the mammoth emerged.

'Is this going to be like Time Lord horse whispering?' asked Amy. 'Are you going to talk to it in its own special language?'

The Doctor shook his head. 'Nah, nothing like that. But tusks and guns – not a good mix.'

Amy nodded her agreement. 'Let's go get our mammoth!'

Together, they bounded through the police cordon and up the steps of the Museum. Above the enormous doors were carved three words: 'Truth', 'Knowledge' and 'Vision'.

The Doctor nudged Amy. 'Also, Mammoths.'

Amy looked up. 'I think I recognise this place from *Grand Theft Auto*.'

As they reached the doors, two armed police officers clad in black pulled the doors back, straining with effort. The Doctor and Amy stepped through, and the doors closed again with a massive clang.

'Plus – when you're going in to face an impossible creature it's best to be absolutely defenceless,' the Doctor remarked conversationally, as if it were an obvious point. 'That way we won't be lulled into a false sense of security.'

'Thought you had a plan?' said Amy. 'You told that lot it would be over in minutes.'

The Doctor grinned at Amy. 'I might have exaggerated the plan part a bit. But don't worry. This is what makes things fun!'

Chapter
3

'Whoa…' the Doctor breathed. 'This is not looking good.'

In front of them, the entrance hall of the Natural History Museum had been trashed beyond recognition. The once spotless polar habitat display was smashed, and its cubes of fake snow were scattered across the marble floor. The neat rows of red chairs had been knocked skewiff as the audience fled, and the massive drapes lay in velvet tatters on the floor. There was no sign of the audience, and heavy wooden and iron doors had been shut all around the huge Grand Hall – locking the miraculous mammoth inside.

Amy heard a heavy clang, and saw that the entrance doors had been closed behind them. They were locked in with a prehistoric monster.

Amy was impressed by the scale of the damage. 'Where is it, then? How can it hide?'

The Doctor scanned the room with his sonic screwdriver. 'Never mind that. Lots of places to go in this Museum… Come on, this way.' He was heading for the edge of the room.

'How do you track a mammoth, anyway?' Amy asked. 'I thought you'd be on your knees using your Time Lord tracker senses or something, listening for mammothy sounds?'

The Doctor was thinking out loud. 'Why would it do this? How could it come back to life? We need to work out the precise order of events, but that's impossible.'

While he was talking, Amy picked up a camera that had been abandoned in the struggle to escape.

'Hey, Time Boy, have a look at this!'

Amy scrolled through the pictures, past grinning shots of a young teacher at a school party, until she reached the unveiling of the mammoth. The first picture showed the hall packed. Some of the same children that had been at the party were grinning brightly. In the second, the man in the white blazer was making a speech.

The next three pictures were of the floor. The final shot made Amy scream with delight. 'Look at this!'

The picture was a close-up of the mammoth's head, in all its wonder. Its jaws were wide open, and

Amy could see row after row of sharp teeth, tusks curving a cruel circle in the air.

The Doctor said nothing. Peeved, Amy looked around and saw him clambering up one of the marble columns, pressing his ear up against the stone. She hurried over.

The Doctor offered Amy his hand. 'Better come up here.'

Amy wasn't impressed. 'Why on earth would I do that? Anyway, I've just found the exact order of events, just like you wanted.'

The Doctor came straight back with: 'I've done better, I've found the mammoth. Now get out of its way.'

Amy turned to follow the Doctor's gaze. But in front of her the hall was empty. 'There's nothing there,' she protested, 'so will you get down from that post! We've got a mammoth to find.'

'Did I not tell you I have very good hearing? Listen through this.'

He leant down and held his screwdriver to Amy's ear. Out of nowhere, a raucous pounding noise filled her ears. Heavy breaths and grunts like nothing she'd ever heard before. It was the panting and stomping of an enormous creature, smashing and howling as it made its way through the Museum. Amplified by the screwdriver, Amy could hear people screaming in horror. An overlapping mix of voices: mums telling children to 'Get back!' Men cursing under their breaths, car horns beeping and mobile phones chattering with the news: 'Oh no, it's coming!'

Amy was lost for words.

'It is a *sonic* screwdriver,' the Doctor explained.

Nervous now, Amy asked, 'How far away is it?'

The Doctor bent his head to one side. 'Not far. I'd say two hundred metres. Or, actually twenty metres. Hard to tell with these things.'

Just as he finished speaking, the glass front of the Museum shop shattered. Glass shards sprayed over the floor, and a huge display of plastic Triceratops exploded, flying through the air. Charging out of the store, souvenir posters and T-Rex T-shirts festooning its massive form, was the wild and frothing mammoth.

The Doctor twiddled his screwdriver, puzzled. 'Glass must have distorted it,' he muttered.

'Never mind that!' Amy yelled. 'It's heading right for me. Pull me up!'

She grabbed the Doctor's hand, and he hauled her up the column, sitting her on top of a window ledge, high above the floor.

She smiled at him. 'Not bad. You're surprisingly strong for a skinny bloke.'

The Doctor looked hurt. 'I am *not* skinny! I'm just you know, not too show-offy about my strength.'

Below them, the mammoth was getting ever nearer, veering from side to side, almost like it was unbalanced. Amy watched it slowing slightly as it reached the centre of the room. She'd never seen anything quite like it.

Next to her, the Doctor was transfixed by the sight. 'Wowzers, that is beautiful!'

Amy shot the Doctor a critical look, mouthing 'wowzers' at him with disdain.

'Yeah, sorry, I'm so not saying that again,' he said. 'Mind you – wowzers. Might catch on…? No?'

Amy shook her head disapprovingly. 'Not likely.'

The Doctor wasn't put off though. 'You have to admit it is beautiful. What a wondrous thing. And it might not even be alien. Could be from your own planet. We could send it back to its own time. Or maybe it'll be happy here. Find it a nice elephant to share its life with—'

'What's it doing?' Amy interrupted. 'It doesn't look very scared.'

From where they were, it almost looked like it was trying to read the calendar in the mess of the gift shop. Amy discounted that as ridiculous.

The Doctor motioned for her to keep quiet, then made a complicated set of hand signals that left her baffled.

'Are you trying to tell me that it'll follow our sounds?' she whispered.

Instantly, the mammoth was on to them, raising its big eyes to gaze at them perched on the window ledge.

The Doctor nodded, then realised there was no point being quiet now. 'They can't see that well, all that hair in their eyes – but just look at those ears!'

'How big do you think it is?'

'I'd say four metres high, probably weighs about ten tonnes, need to eat a lot to keep up that kind of energy.' He noticed Amy's reaction. 'I didn't mean to say the wrong thing about eating. They don't eat humans, far as I know, not that I've met one before, I'll just stop now, OK?'

Looking decidedly angry, and smashing a path through the seats, the mammoth was heading straight for their vantage point. Amy felt very exposed. They were in the centre of the mammoth's path, high and dry, with no way of escape.

Acting tough in the face of danger, Amy went on. 'A little beastie like that? You've fought off worse. In fact, I've fought off meaner-looking things in Leadworth. If the caveman can get rid of it, then surely we can?'

The Doctor looked straight at Amy Pond. He was half proud of her and half scared. Amy was confident beyond her abilities, ready to leap into any situation whatever it meant, and full of absolute trust in him.

'You are brilliant, Amy Pond,' he said, 'but there's a thing. A very important thing. A thing that's been troubling me for the last five minutes. This mammoth has survived two ice ages, the Stone Age, the Bronze

Age, the Iron Age, the nuclear age. So how has it managed that when almost nothing else has? Maybe it's because it's the most vicious mammoth in all of creation, so bloodthirsty it survived. Or maybe it's because it's so wise and peaceful no one has ever wanted to harm it, and it has been kept safe and protected for thousands and thousands of years. Or, and I'm not making a speech this long again, especially halfway up a marble column, *or* – it's not a mammoth at all. Which leads me to think it's drawing the attention of the world to it, so maybe it's just a mistake? Or, or, or it could be a diversion and, while I'm here, Washington is being turned into a spa town for insect creatures. Either way, we need to stop it before anyone else does…'

'Sshhh!' Amy was calm and focused.

The mighty mammoth was almost directly below them now. She could hear its every breath and pant. Something in it was rumbling and growling, a noise so deep and so primal it would have stilled the assault of any predator.

The Doctor continued regardless. 'Whatever it is, it's trapped in a museum with five hundred innocent people, and we can't allow it to reach them. We need to get it out the door, where your new admirers can tranquillise—'

Amy interrupted him again. 'Before you do that, Doctor, would you mind telling me why it's safer up here?'

The Doctor looked at Amy as if she was crackers. 'Safer? It's not safer up here. We came up here to make it easier to get onto it.'

Amy was filled with horror. 'Onto it? Are you mental? I thought we were staying out of its way.'

The Doctor was calm and pragmatic. 'No, it would be far safer down there, here we're on its level.'

Only metres away from them, the mammoth raised its head, and its huge eyes looked right at them, its brutal tusks almost touching their legs.

Why did doing what the Doctor said ever seem like a good idea, Amy wondered. 'You know Doctor,' she said, 'I've never taken orders from a bloke before.'

The Doctor smiled. 'Ah, but then again, you never got to do this!' With a yell of: 'Geronimo!' he swung Amy off the window ledge, and the two of them landed straight on the back of the mammoth.

Chapter
4

Digging his hands into the mammoth's thick white coat, the Doctor leant over and yelled in Amy's ear, 'Hang on! It's going to be a bumpy ride.'

Amy curled her fingers into the mammoth's hair and clung on as the beast thundered around the Grand Hall of the Museum.

'It's a bit like horse-riding,' the Doctor yelled.

'I've only been once, I broke my arm,' she replied.

'Well let's hope you learned,' the Doctor shouted back.

'Never went bullfighting, though,' Amy yelled.

'Bullfighting?'

She pointed ahead, almost losing her balance. 'Looks like that's what he's doing!'

In front of them, a man had stepped out into the hall. He was wearing what had once been a strikingly white blazer, which was now stained and torn. Amy recognised him from the footage of the mammoth breaking loose.

The Doctor had obviously recognised the man too, because he yelled in Amy's ear, 'Look, he's OK.'

Amy twisted round to see the man standing proud in the middle of the hall.

'Oh no,' the Doctor continued. 'I think he's trying to knock it out... with a wooden chair.'

The man was waving and shouting to attract the mammoth's attention, and was hopelessly trying to hide a chair behind his back.

'Oi, hairy!' the man yelled. Within seconds, the mammoth had changed direction and was heading straight for him.

'Get out of the way!' Amy cried, not quite able to believe the man was even attempting this. She saw him take the chair from behind his back and raise it above his head, all set to smash it on the runaway creature.

Acting quickly, the Doctor aimed his sonic screwdriver and directed a quick burst at the chair, which fell apart in the man's hands.

'Why did you do that?' Amy asked.

'No point getting it any angrier,' the Doctor replied.

Weaponless and surprised, the man turned to run, but the mammoth now had a new target: the door to the rest of the Museum. It headed at full pelt for the locked door.

'Duck!' the Doctor yelled.

In an explosion of splinters and broken wood panels, the mammoth broke free of the Grand Hall and charged down a marble corridor. It roared as it raced through the hall of the Age of Man, sending the skeleton of a three-million-year-old woman clattering to the floor with a thrust of its tusks. Then it slowed to gaze at the vast diorama of Neanderthal man and a picture of a relatively small brown mammoth.

The Doctor was looking around with interest. 'This is the best way to see museums. It gets it over with so much quicker!'

He had ended up sitting behind Amy on the beast's back and was now hanging onto her waist as the white mammoth skittered round the marble floors, his legs flailing out to one side.

Amy shouted back, 'What you doing?'

The Doctor didn't answer – he was too busy trying to stop himself slipping off. Amy reached back and grabbed him by his braces, yanking him back up on top of the mammoth.

'Hah, I never thought I'd be thankful you're wearing those braces,' she said. 'Thought you'd be OK sitting on this with those bandy legs of yours.'

The Doctor looked rattled. 'What do you mean?'

Amy grinned at him. 'Haven't you ever looked in a full-length mirror? You could ride a horse between those!'

As the mammoth thundered along another corridor, the Doctor leaned forward as far as he could, and aimed his sonic screwdriver at the mammoth's ears.

'It's not working,' he yelled back to Amy. Hanging on with one hand, he fiddled with the device and tried again.

'What's not working?'

'There's a thing you can do to some animals, makes them relax, like stroking a dog, or turning a rabbit on its back.'

'And that was your plan, was it?'

If anything, the mammoth seemed to have become more erratic, not less.

'Thing is,' the Doctor explained, 'it should work on a mammoth. Something's not right.'

'What do you mean?' she asked.

The mammoth abruptly changed direction, and the Doctor began to slip again. Amy had to yank him back on. She looked back up to see that they were now heading full-pelt for a massive whale skeleton.

The Doctor had seen it too. 'Got to be able to steer this thing. I told Commander Strebbins we'd bring it out under control…'

Amy was flabbergasted. 'There is no way you can steer a mammoth!'

The Doctor leant forward and put Amy's hands on the neck of mammoth. It felt warm and powerful under her hands. 'Just pull to the left and see what happens.'

'You are impossible!' Amy shouted. She'd imagined travelling around New York in style, and here she was trying to steer a prehistoric animal around the New York Natural History Museum.

Amy gripped the animal tight and pulled the mammoth's neck to the left with all of her might. The mammoth wailed in outrage, and spun rapidly to the right. They smashed through the blue whale's tail, sending bones flying through the air.

Amy wasn't amused. 'I think it's trying to shake us off.'

Increasingly enraged by its unwanted passengers, the mammoth was now heading for a replica cave. The top was so low the mammoth was barely going to squeeze through it…

'Can't you steer it away?' the Doctor asked.

I am so *going to get you back for this*, thought Amy.

The Doctor yelled 'Duck!' and Amy flattened herself on the animal's back as it galloped through the cave. They made it through to the other side where the mammoth hurtled into a display of penguins, toppling them like dominoes.

Amy blinked, her mind distracted, confused by something. 'Are there any Nile Penguins here?'

The Doctor stared at her like she was mad. 'They don't exist, Amy. That's a myth. What made you think of them?'

Amy wasn't sure. For a brief moment, it had felt like a long-forgotten memory had burst urgently back into her life, but it had departed just as quickly, and she had no idea why she'd thought it was important. 'I just had such a weird feeling of déjà vu,' she said.

'That's just echoes of memories,' the Doctor told her cheerily. 'Reverberating down your timeline, nothing to worry about. Unless it's déjà vu of you wetting yourself. You haven't, have you?'

Amy laughed. The Doctor had an amazing ability to make the scariest things feel fun, and the worst times become the best. She wanted to hug him, but realised they were about to hit another doorway.

Amy and the Doctor ducked down close to the mammoth's fur again. When they sat back up, they were in the glorious light of the Hall of Diamonds. Amy was dazzled. She'd never imagined such enormous jewels existed.

'Maybe this is a robbery?' Amy yelled at the Doctor. 'A very clever robbery…'

'I don't think so…' the Doctor replied.

He was still lying on the mammoth's back, and was listening intently to something. He gestured for

Amy to bend down with him. 'Tell me if I'm wrong, but that doesn't sound like an animal to me…'

Amy couldn't tell for sure but, through the fur and warmth of the animal, she thought she could hear the *click-click-click* of cogs turning.

The Doctor took his sonic screwdriver out and pointed it at the mammoth's back leg. It whirred and the mammoth's leg gave way with a *FATOOM!* Amy clung to the fur as, for a second, it seemed like the creature was going to collapse. With a mighty effort, the mammoth hauled its leg back up.

'That's interesting.' The Doctor was tapping at the mammoth's back. 'This is real muscle and real fur, held on in a real way.' He tugged a bit of white fur loose, and the mammoth wailed. 'See, it really hurts.'

Amy rolled her eyes at him. 'Well, durrr.'

'But underneath this real animal,' the Doctor continued, 'there's a metal skeleton…'

'So we can switch it off?'

The Doctor looked worried. If the mammoth had been built, then this was going to get complicated… How could he know what was going to hurt the beast? Like a little boy, he desperately wanted to take it apart and see how it worked, but he couldn't be sure how much was machine and how much was animal.

With all four legs working again, the mammoth put on a burst of speed and they crashed past a giant canoe, arriving back where they'd started in the Great Hall.

The doors had been hauled open, presumably so the Doctor and Amy could lead the mammoth out as they had promised. Seeing its chance to escape, the mammoth bellowed with triumph and charged for freedom...

Bursting out into daylight, the mammoth paused. It was built for arctic plains and vicious tussles with other bloodthirsty animals, but outside everything was concrete and brick and flashing lights. In that brief moment, the mammoth was hit with a barrage of tranquilliser darts.

'Will the tranquillisers work on it?' Amy asked.

There was no reply, and she twisted round to look behind her. The Doctor was sound asleep. He had been struck in the leg by a dart and had flopped onto the mammoth's back.

'Wake up!' Amy screamed at him in frustration.

The mammoth was about to tumble over and they were still on its back. Amy grabbed the Doctor and pulled him to one side as the mammoth staggered and then collapsed on the steps.

Surrounded by New Yorkers and live on TV, Amy stood beside the sleeping body of the mammoth, the Doctor in her arms – and heard a huge cheer. Smiling, Amy waved at the crowds. They'd only stopped off for a burger, but they'd managed to catch a mammoth. She slid down off the back of the beast, and several men clad in severe black clothes grabbed both of her arms.

Officer Oscar Henderson stepped up to her, a grim look on his face. He snapped a pair of cuffs around her wrists, and motioned for her to 'zip it' when Amy opened her mouth to complain.

'I think it's time you two came with us,' he said.

Chapter
5

Oscar Henderson had been working for Commander Strebbins for six months, and he'd never seen her like this before. He guessed that she was feeling out of her depth. He knew she had spent twenty years in the Baltimore City Police, working her way up from foot patrols on the roughest streets, to become Chief of the entire district.

A new unit was being set up to deal with Serious Civil Unrest. They needed a hard nut to run it, someone who wouldn't be scared by whatever the city had to throw at her – and someone who'd stay calm, whatever was happening. In the last two years, Strebbins had coped with riots on the streets, striking taxi drivers and bomb threats. But the mammoth was something new, and Oscar could see that Strebbins was absolutely fuming. She paced up and down in front of her lieutenants, barking orders.

'I want every single person in the Museum interviewed. I want names, I want backgrounds, I want witness statements. If one of them so much as farts out of turn, send them to me! And most of all, get me the Man in the White Jacket!'

The other officers filed out of Strebbins's office, their mission clear, but Oscar heard his name and stepped back inside her office. Strebbins shut the door behind him, conspiratorial.

'Now we're alone, I need to tell you something.'

Oscar sat down but, seeing that Strebbins stayed standing, he awkwardly got to his feet again and stood in the centre of the room while Strebbins paced her office.

'I'm going to tell you about the man with the silly hair we let into the Museum. What I have to say must remain top secret. I'm telling you as you're being assigned to deal with him and his friend.'

Oscar couldn't tell whether this was going to be a good or bad thing yet. 'She's called Amy Pond,' he confided. 'Scottish police force.'

'She's nothing of the sort,' Strebbins snapped back. 'The man is called the Doctor. The code he used to gain access has been on record since 1932. The origins are vague, but I'm instructed to step aside to the bearer of the code, and allow them to pursue their actions. However harebrained those actions might seem.'

Strebbins paused for a moment. This obviously wasn't the kind of conversation she wanted to be having with a junior officer. Oscar usually saw her barking direct orders at them and going home to her dogs.

'That was actually in the wording of the command,' Strebbins went on. '*However harebrained those actions might seem.* Now, I'm in charge of this city's response to major threats. And I consider the intrusion of a mammoth to be one of them. It was a mistake to let the man in the tweed jacket into the Museum. I hold myself responsible, and I'm certainly not going to repeat it. I give my authority to no one. So I need a solution. Since this young man arrived in town, things have started to go wrong. I can smell trouble, but this time I can't stop it. Colonel Mace from UNIT is on his way here from Vancouver, and I want this wrapped up before he gets here. I start to need help in my own backyard, pretty soon we'll all be shut down. I want you to stay on their case. Wherever the Doctor goes, you go, whatever they do, I want you to be there with them.'

Oscar smiled. This sounded like a promotion to him. He couldn't wait to tell the rest of the boys that he was on the personal instructions of the Commander.

'One thing, Henderson,' Strebbins continued. 'I

can't have this being reported. You know how this place works. It's all time sheets and duty logs and explaining ourselves to a higher authority. I'm not having any of that. You'll take the next few days as leave. If you want to ring in, I'm giving you my personal cell phone number.' She handed Oscar a blank card with a number written on it in biro.

'Thank you, ma'am. This is a great honour.'

Strebbins cut him off. 'Can it, Oscar. You're doing this 'cos you're the only guy here that the girl talked to. I need you to get close in to them. So lose the grateful act.'

Oscar was smiling as he left the office. If taking care of the two eccentrics was all he had to do, he was going to have an easy time of it.

Strebbins was obviously more concerned than Oscar. She punched a speed-dial button on her desk phone.

'This is Commander Strebbins. Status update on the apprehended creature, please.'

Oscar could hear the reply through the speakerphone: 'It's out cold. We're clearing the dog pound for it. Until then, it stays on the flatbed.'

'Forget the dog pound,' Strebbins ordered. 'This thing needs proper protection. Take it to the zoo.'

'Are you sure?' queried the duty officer.

Strebbins's lower lip trembled with anger. 'If I hear you haven't done it, you're fired.'

*

Ever since the sleeping mammoth had been taken away by the cops, Sam Horwitz had been hiding deep in the basement of the Natural History Museum. He'd seen how quickly the ginger girl had been handcuffed, and he had slipped quietly back into the Museum in the hubbub. He knew he'd have to face his fate sooner or later, but for now he was trying to piece together the mystery of the mammoth. Working furiously at his desk, he'd been going through every scan and test he had run on the mammoth. It had been improbable enough that the beast still had fur when he first found it, let alone that it could breathe. He sighed, and put his head in his hands.

This wasn't how the day had been meant to go. By now, he thought, he should have been interviewed countless times on television and radio, answering questions in as many languages as the world spoke. He would have answered humbly and calmly, explaining how he alone had found and preserved the mammoth. Then, after an exhausting but triumphant day, he would have asked Polly Vernon out to dinner. Tired, but sparkling, she would have seen in him what he saw in her, and all the months of working alone would have been worth it.

Now, instead, his career was over. In the space of a few minutes, he'd gone from being the rising star of Palaeontology to the biggest booby in all of America. He'd brought a living creature into the sacred heart of the Natural History Museum and let it loose on hundreds of people. Priceless displays had been destroyed, and the two strangers that had leapt upon its back had almost been killed.

He couldn't stop remembering Polly's face asking him what she should do. It was so obvious to him now that he should have led her and her school to safety. That's what a hero would have done. Instead, he'd told her to run, and tried to talk to a mammoth. Some kind of hero he was.

But even through all of this, part of him couldn't get over how incredible it all was. His dreams of seeing living specimens of magnificent animals from the past had come true. He'd never imagined he would know how it felt to have the breath of a mammoth on his cheeks, or to quake in fear as one stampeded along the corridor. Sam thought that this must be how the cavemen had felt. He had seen new dangers in the world, and emerged unscathed.

There was a timid knock on the door, and Sam's evening of woe instantly got a whole lot better. Polly Vernon was at the door, smiling brightly.

'Is it safe to come in?' she asked.

Sam laughed, so relieved to see a good friend like Polly. Even better, she was carrying boxes of Chinese takeaway.

'Thought I might find you here...' she went on. 'Maybe we can just stay in tonight? Out of everyone's way.'

Sam couldn't help but give Polly an enormous hug. He'd turned his cell phone off after the hundredth news crews rang for the thousandth time. All demanding interviews and statements. 'Was this a hoax?' 'Where was it found?' 'Who is responsible?'

Sam had turned on the TV earlier – only to see himself facing down a mammoth, and the Director of the Museum talking sternly to camera about the internal investigation to be launched, and saying plainly and pointedly that this was the brainchild of one of their junior colleagues – Sam Horwitz.

'What are they saying out there?' Sam asked Polly.

She looked at the floor. 'Don't you worry about them, they'll calm down. No one was hurt, that's the important thing.'

'Except the Barosaurus,' Sam said glumly.

Polly nodded. 'Yes, but that's been dead for millions of years, so no one counts it.'

Sam was so pleased Polly was there. But he had to ask her. 'Are you disappointed in me?' He could feel his eyes welling up with tears and blinked them back.

Polly said nothing. She just opened her arms, and gave him a big hug. 'It wasn't your fault,' she said eventually. 'Who could have known they were able to survive hibernation like that?'

'I'm so sorry, Polly. I was so scared.'

Polly was shaking her head. 'Today, you were the bravest man I've ever seen. That thing is one crazy animal. It can probably eat a Tyrannosaurus Rex before breakfast, and you went toe to toe with it! You didn't even run. I was so proud of you.'

'But it's all my fault,' Sam moaned.

'You tried to get everyone to be calm. There were five hundred people in that room, and only one person thought of saving everyone else. You.'

Sam felt the happiest he'd been in hours. Maybe it wasn't going to be so bad. Even though he knew his time in the Museum was over and he'd be lucky to get a job teaching fourth graders, he was proud that he had friends like Polly.

'So, Mr Explorer,' Polly was saying, 'I think it's time you told me where on Earth you found that monstrosity. I thought you'd been eaten by moths or something you'd spent so much time at work. Now I know you were keeping this secret. No wonder I didn't see you for so long.'

Sam realised that the burden of the secret was lifted and he no longer had to hide. For the first time in months he felt able to tell Polly the truth.

When he'd first met Polly, Sam's life had been very different. He'd been a lowly research assistant and, for all his jokes and games, he had been learning to forget his dreams. As a boy, Sam had always loved reading about prehistoric creatures and imagining what the past was like. He dreamed of seeing the days when Tyrannosaurus Rex ruled the world, and when herds of Diplodocus grazed the vast plains. But after months of boring work in the Museum he had thought that he would never get to be an adventurer, or to blaze his own trail through undiscovered mountains and dangerous jungles.

But then, one day, while he was cataloguing reindeer droppings, he had found a piece of paper tucked inside an old map of Svalbard. It had claimed to be the location of a hidden treasure of dinosaur bones, buried beneath hundreds of metres of Arctic ice, high in the icy plains of Svalbard.

The notes on the edge of the map claimed that dinosaurs had gathered around a volcanic spring to shelter from the last ice age, only to be trapped when the ice sheets advanced. Dinosaurs from all over the continent had gathered around the oasis of warm water and, as the longest winter crept in, the dinosaurs had been frozen deep down under the glaciers. If the story was right, the dinosaurs would have been frozen so quickly, and kept in conditions so cold, that they would be the best preserved dinosaurs ever. And if the map was right, there would be types of dinosaur in the hidden valley that no one had ever seen before.

So when Sam had heard there was a spare place on an Arctic mission he knew it was too good an opportunity to miss. Whilst his colleagues were labelling whale bones in Stockholm Museum, he had set off with two huskies and a warm coat to search for the mysterious Dinosaur Oasis and its treasures. They had all thought he was mad.

But Sam had surprised them all when he'd returned to Stockholm, his borrowed fishing boat weighed down with a very unusual cargo. Sam Horwitz had found the first ever Polar Woolly Mammoth.

Standing four metres tall, its tusks were two metres long, and it's eyes the size of dinner plates. Its teeth were long and still sharp, unblemished by the years in the cold, and its muscles still rippled, preserved in all their might and glory. The beast had a coat of pure white fur, and a mouth as wide as a car. It was truly fearsome to behold. And Sam had found it.

The mammoth had been shipped back to New York in great secrecy. Sam hadn't told Polly because he knew she'd have wanted to see it. And he knew if even a few people saw it – even Polly – the secret would get out.

They'd been successful in keeping the mammoth under wraps and, until this fateful day, hardly anyone had seen it. Rumours had spread around the Museum of what Sam was working on. People had speculated that he'd found the 'missing link' of the chain of Evolution, or that he'd found a new kind of prehistoric human skeleton.

But now the creature had turned out to be

something entirely different. And Sam desperately wanted to do something to put right what he had done.

Chapter
6

When Oscar arrived at the Midtown Police Station, he was horrified to find most of the uniformed police were standing outside drinking cups of takeaway coffee.

'What are you doing?' he asked, finding it hard to believe they were all outside.

'We're on orders from Scotland Yard,' an older cop answered. 'Girl with red hair, she was very insistent we wait outside. Nice girl though, she bought us all these.' The cop nodded to a big box of doughnuts, most of which had been eaten.

Oscar cursed and ran to the main doors, only to find the front desk was shut down and the police station locked.

'They can't lock me out of a police station!' he

yelled. But it seemed that they could.

Keeping an eye on the Doctor was going to be harder than Oscar had imagined.

The Doctor woke up behind bars. He was lying on a metal bunk in a New York Police Department cell.

On the wall beside him, someone had scratched what looked like a tally of years. For a short moment, the Doctor panicked. Had he been in the cell for that long? Where was Amy? Still cloudy from the tranquilliser, he couldn't quite piece together the last few hours.

A familiar voice broke his thoughts.

'Oi, Dozy of Alcatraz!'

The delicate sound of Amy Pond brought a smile to the Doctor's face. She was standing at the cell door with a bored expression.

'Do you have any idea how long I've been waiting for you?' she went on. 'It's not like they have magazines in the waiting room here. You missed the best bit: me, a box of doughnuts and twelve skinny lattes, and the NYPD were mine for the taking. You should have seen me, I was pretty impressive. Anyway, looks like New York has taken a shine to the mammoth.'

She unfurled a copy of the *New York Times* and held it up to the hatch so the Doctor could see the front page headline: 'New York Welcomes Woolly the Mammoth'.

The Doctor sprang to his feet, instantly tense. 'Right, we've got to get to it. Er... how long have I been here, then?'

'I was coming to that...' Amy told him. 'I thought you'd have woken up earlier, being all Super-Human Time Lord and all that...'

The Doctor counted the number of holes in his trousers. 'They hit me with six tranquilliser darts. Even two hearts take a while to get rid of that kind of dose. I must have been asleep for... No!'

With a sense of dread, the Doctor looked at the time. Six hours. He'd been asleep for six hours. He rattled the door of the cell. 'We have to get out of here!' Pulling himself up on the window ledge he could see that the sun was setting. 'Oh no, no, no, no, no.'

Amy told him to calm down. 'Woolly is safe in the zoo, all behind bars. Job done. Us one, mammoths nil.'

The Doctor wasn't ready to celebrate. 'We must be too late... We need to get to it...' He realised he wasn't making much sense to Amy and launched into a passionate explanation. 'I know what's wrong with the mammoth! When I was on its back I could hear it, and beneath the muscle and the sweat there was another noise. There was a ticking, and a clanking of old machinery getting back into action. The mammoth isn't real. It's a fake. A giant mechanical creature, disguised to look like a vicious prehistoric animal.'

Amy was quiet for a moment. 'I read somewhere that all the dinosaurs and prehistoric animals were fakes—' she said.

The Doctor cut her off. 'Nah, I've been there. Lovely caves, beautiful sunsets in those days. They were definitely real. But this is something else, and more than that – it's unprotected, and it's right in the middle of New York.'

'But who would make something like that?' Amy asked.

'I don't know,' the Doctor answered impatiently, pacing the cell with frustration. 'But I need to find out. Unless the cavemen got *very* clever without me noticing, something from another planet or another time hid the mammoth under the ice.' The Doctor gestured at Amy to hurry up. 'So come on, Pond, can't you pick the lock with a hairpin, or something? I need to get out of here!'

Amy smiled. 'I've got an easier way. C'mere, Brad.'

In the corridor outside the cell, a handsome clean-cut police officer walked over to the door and winked at Amy. 'Not leaving already are you?'

Amy charmed him with ease. 'Me and my dozy friend are off now. Your boss said he was OK to go as soon as he could walk.'

Brad peered in at the Doctor, who was doing his best to look harmless. 'He looks kind of weird to me, but whatever floats your boat.'

With a smile, Amy whisked the electronic key tag off Brad's belt and pressed it up against the door. With a loud clunk, the door to the cell slid open, and the Doctor stepped out. He promptly tripped over his boots.

Brad looked at him with visible disdain.

'Right, first shoelaces,' the Doctor decided. 'Then let's go! We need to get to the mammoth. And fast.'

While the Doctor had been asleep, Amy had watched as the massive mammoth was loaded onto a flatbed truck and transported across town to the New York City Zoo.

'Right now,' Amy told the Doctor, 'the mammoth is sleeping happily between the rhinos and the elephants. They're going to get a surprise when it wakes up.'

The Doctor looked distressed. 'Oh, Amy, you should have woken *me* up…'

Amy was disappointed. She'd done her very best without the Doctor and had hoped he would have noticed more of what she'd managed to do. 'Hang on, I stopped them carting you off to the Gotham Asylum, or whatever they have here, and I convinced them I was the only person fit to look after you. Professor of Psychology at Oxford no less. And Special Inspector with Scotland Yard, Flying Squad. So less of the grumpy face.'

The Doctor smiled sympathetically. 'You're right. Sorry. You've been brilliant. But our days of working with the NYPD are over, Professor Pond. Far better we do things our own way from now on. The right way. Follow me. I'll show you how it's done.'

They found a rear exit and walked out of the station into a backyard full of rubbish bins. Beyond the bins, squad cars and riot vans were parked up, ready to take out on patrol for the night shift.

The Doctor grinned at Amy. 'I've always wanted to drive one of these!'

Amy held him back. 'We can't steal a police car!'

The Doctor wasn't deterred. 'First the clothes, now this. Next you'll be telling me to take the TARDIS back to whoever I borrowed it off.'

Amy wasn't convinced. 'I'm an honorary member of the NYPD, anyway. Well, maybe.'

Leaping into the driver's seat, the Doctor soniced the ignition, and the engine roared into life. 'Come on, Amy!'

Amy got into the squad car. 'I suppose it's nice to see one of these from the front seat.'

Oscar ran round to the back of the station, just in time to see the Doctor and Amy drive off. He resisted the urge to call in and get the car pulled over. Strebbins had told him to do this quietly.

Instead, he called in to Brad that he was taking a car. After signing four forms and a health disclaimer,

Oscar headed off after the Doctor and Amy.

It wasn't difficult to work out where they were going. They wanted the mammoth, and he knew exactly where to find them.

Chapter
7

The sun was setting over New York. The Doctor left the squad car parked on Fifth Avenue, and Amy took a moment to take in the beauty and sheer scale of Central Park. Above her, ducks circled lazily, and thousands of lights were being switched on across the city, making the steel and glass towers glow against the sky.

'Wow!' Amy was impressed. 'On the maps, the park looks tiny. But you could fit all of Leadworth into it. Twice.'

The Doctor signalled for Amy to be quiet as they got within sight of the Zoo. As the evening drew in, the Zoo was shutting down for the night, and the main entrance was full of groups of schoolchildren, filing out as the security guards closed up.

'Where exactly *is* the Zoo?' the Doctor asked.

Before Amy could speak, he answered his own question.

'It's right in the middle of New York, isn't it…'

'Does that mean anything?' Amy asked.

'We're about to find out.'

They circled the Zoo fence until they reached the service gates. Beyond the heavy steel doors, they could see the top of the large animal enclosure, tantalisingly close.

'I can sonic the gates open,' the Doctor told Amy, 'but I'm gonna need a diversion…'

He nodded towards the entrance. On either side of the service gates, two security guards were sitting back in their chairs, chatting and laughing.

Amy smiled and whispered to the Doctor, 'I've got a really good idea. You stop here, I'll get them out of the way.'

The Doctor crouched on the ground as Amy crawled across the road and ducked behind a bush. A moment later a tiny pebble skittered along the tarmac and came to rest beside the foot of the security guard. The man didn't notice and kept on talking to the other guard.

Amy tried again, with a slightly larger stone. This time it bounced up, and knocked against the guard's knee. But he still didn't notice. The Doctor signalled to Amy that they didn't have much time.

On her third attempt, Amy chucked a hefty stone.

It flew through the air, bounced off the ground, and whacked the guard right on the forehead.

'Owww!' cried the guard. Putting his hand to his head he fell back off his seat, crying in pain for a second time as he landed heavily on the ground. Concerned, the other security guard rushed over to his side.

Amy was sure she could see tears rolling down the guard's cheek as he rubbed his sore head. She ran back to the Doctor's side.

The Doctor asked, 'Was *that* your really good idea? I thought maybe you'd cause a clever scene, or something, not whack him on the head.'

Amy rolled her eyes. 'Enough with the criticism. Your turn now.'

The Doctor raised an eyebrow at Amy, not impressed at all.

'I'm sorry, all right,' she said. 'I panicked. You were pressuring me. I didn't mean to make him cry.' She paused, and added: 'Looks like they're off, though.'

Sure enough, both guards were heading off to get first aid, one of them still visibly upset.

'Don't you dare stop asking me to do this stuff though,' Amy continued. 'I'm good at this. Just you wait and see.'

As she spoke, Amy slipped in a large pile of elephant dung. She glared up at the Doctor, who backed away laughing.

'I'm not saying anything,' he told her. 'Look at me, not saying anything. See me, absolutely not pointing at you and laughing.'

Amy tried to ignore him. 'Hurry up. They're distracted, aren't they? Come on. Sonic away. Get those locks open. Let's go!'

While Amy cleaned herself up, the Doctor clicked the screwdriver and, with a thunder crack, the doors of the Zoo blew open with an enormous bang.

The Doctor grinned, looking stupidly pleased with himself. 'I didn't know it could do that! Sonic energy excites the hydrocarbons in the oil in the hinges, and – Boom! Instant access. Just look at it.'

Amy was aghast. 'All of New York will have heard that! What was the point of me distracting them?'

'You've been in Leadworth too long, Amy Pond. Big city like this, they'll think it's someone celebrating New Year. Always a New Year for someone…'

Inside the Zoo, the elephants were uneasy. Flappy the Elephant (named by a children's TV programme) had been perplexed when his usual afternoon visit had been abandoned and men clad in black baseball hats had unloaded a strange and new kind of animal.

Flappy had learnt to be glad whenever new animals arrived, especially elephants. He'd been a bit lonely since Elephunk the Musical Elephant had gone to Philadelphia Zoo, and he wanted someone to talk trunk to trunk with. But this new animal was different...

The zookeepers hadn't been pleased when it arrived. There had been shouting and screaming and tones of voice Flappy normally only heard if the goat's head butted a child. And then when he had finally seen the creature unloaded, he'd been deeply suspicious.

It wasn't the colour that seemed odd: in his short life, Flappy had seen creatures of all kinds go past. It was the *smell*. The new woolly thing in the next cage smelt *clean*, almost like it was new. It didn't smell like an actual animal. It smelt more like a load of washing, or the boiler suits worn by the keepers every second Monday. Flappy had tried to communicate this to his favourite keeper, but she'd simply given his trunk a rub and fed him a banana. And now that the woolly creature had woken up, it was behaving even more oddly, pawing at the ground, and walking in strange concentric circles.

Flappy wasn't to know, but the Polar Woolly Mammoth was doing something very akin to pacing out the dimensions of the cage.

Chapter

8

The Doctor and Amy crouched low and stepped quietly into the Zoo. The locks were red hot and smoking in the evening air. To get to the enclosures they had to sidle past a little hut where the crying security guard was holding an ice pack to his bruised head while his friend was busy putting plasters on his injuries.

Safely past the hut, the Doctor and Amy ducked off the main track and crept along behind the enclosures. This was the secret part of the Zoo where the keepers stored the animal food and the old, smelly hay. These shortcuts from the main path zigzagged through the Zoo, and unwittingly the Doctor and Amy stumbled out onto one of the main walkways.

As a crowd of naughty school children went past, Amy saw someone headed straight for them and pulled the Doctor back. She was too late: a zookeeper returning from her rounds stopped to talk to the Doctor.

'Hey, mister, nice bow tie.'

The Doctor turned to Amy, grinning triumphantly. 'See! I told you it was cool. Just you wait and see, they'll all be wearing them soon.'

Amy pointed over the Doctor's shoulder where the keeper was still waiting to talk to the Doctor…

'School visiting time is over now, sir,' the keeper continued. 'Would you be so kind as to fetch your class from the petting zoo. It's closing time.'

Amy struggled to keep a straight face. The keeper thought that the Doctor was a teacher.

The Doctor smiled and tried to explain himself. 'Ah, right, you think I'm a teacher 'cos of the jacket and the bow tie, ah, I think you'll see their teacher is actually over there.' He pointed to the other side of the path, where a flustered-looking man was having a sneaky cigarette by the koala cage.

The teacher was a deeply uncool man in his forties, flustered, paunchy and wearing a purple shirt and bow tie. He was trying very hard to ignore the noise of the rowdy children who were meant to be in his care.

Amy laughed out loud. 'You could so be brothers.'

The keeper pointed down the path. 'Thank you both. The exit is that way.'

Amy held her hands up as the keeper walked away. 'I am saying nothing. That was just priceless.'

'Yeah, quiet, Pond. Just keep walking…'

The Doctor and Amy followed the keeper's instructions until they were out of sight, then ducked down another back alley. The service path weaved in and out of the animal enclosures and made the Zoo look like a crazy mass of concrete walls, bars and piles of animal dung.

'Where do you put a mammoth in a place like this?' Amy asked.

'Follow me,' said the Doctor, striding off down the dusty path.

As the light faded, and the last visitors left, the Zoo became dominated by the excitable chattering of wildlife. Macaque monkeys squabbled in the trees, gnus lounged in the long grass and, safe from view, polar bears did energetic laps of their pool, throwing pieces of fish to each other as if they were playing water polo.

As they walked, the Doctor told Amy the best way to deal with wild animals. 'In a place like this they're all well fed, so you've no real need to worry. Out in the wild there is one very important thing to remember. You need to make sure you look as little like *food* as possible.'

'Is that it?' Amy said. 'Grrrreat. Top advice.'

The Doctor pointed to a crocodile, and they both went very quiet.

Tiptoeing past, the Doctor whispered to Amy when they were well clear of the reptile. 'I don't think he remembered me... Never do a deal with a crocodile, Amy. They tend to eat the contract.'

Amy laughed. 'You expect me to believe everything.'

Finally, they reached the large animal enclosure. The mammoth's cage had been clumsily covered with white plastic sheets, and a double fence closed the area off.

The Doctor looked at Amy. 'One more chance. Keep out signs are like a red rag to a bull for you. I'm sure you can get through here.'

Amy grinned, stepped forward, casually lifted the fence from its support, and stepped through the gap. 'I've never paid for a festival yet.'

Pushing up the bars, the Doctor tore the white plastic sheet down, and found himself face to face with the Polar Woolly Mammoth.

'Whoa! It must have been watching us through the sheets. That's some eyesight it's got.' The Doctor took his sonic screwdriver out and shone it into the mammoth's eyes.

'This is beautiful work,' he said. 'Exceptional. It must have taken years to make an iris and a pupil that work as well as this. And the tusks! Yep, hardened dead hair, definitely real.'

'So what's fake about it?' Amy asked. As she did, the mammoth let rip a fart. 'That *smells* pretty real to me.'

The Doctor was staring absentmindedly into the distance. 'I wonder...' He fiddled with his sonic screwdriver and shone a green light onto the mammoth's fur.

Where the beam touched the fur, the light seemed to linger, as if the sonic screwdriver had caused the fur to glow.

'What are you doing, Doctor?' Amy asked.

The Doctor was too focused on his task to answer. 'This is just amazing...' Swinging up on the bars of the enclosure, the Doctor stood above the beast, and lit the mammoth with a large torch. All of the creature was glowing a mysterious green, phosphorescent in the dark of the Zoo.

'Where did you get that from?' Amy wondered, looking at the torch.

'Big pockets. Not really relevant at the moment.'

'You want me to ask about the fur?'

'It's not fur. Can't be. Ordinary fur doesn't glow. And not just with the sonic, it's any light source that sets it off. Whatever else is real about this, the fur definitely isn't. Looks like some kind of nano-fibre-optic technology, something that certainly wasn't around in the mammoth's time.'

'Unless all the mammoths were alien robots,' Amy suggested.

The Doctor grinned. 'I'll take you there some day, you can find out for yourself.' As he spoke, he was fiddling with his sonic screwdriver, and a beam of light shone into the mammoth's ear, which began to twitch bizarrely.

'Ha! I've got it! But I think this is about to get very embarrassing indeed.'

The Doctor leapt down into the enclosure with the mammoth, and opened the gate from the inside to let Amy in. He kept talking as he shut it carefully behind her. 'Very, very embarrassing. I expect they'll be blushing when they have to explain themselves.'

'Tell me what you mean.' Amy gave him a friendly punch on the arm. Although not so friendly it didn't hurt him a bit. 'Hey, spaceman, you're not making sense!'

Rubbing his shoulder, the Doctor went on. 'Sorry, sorry, am I talking out of sequence again? So many things in my head sometimes they just come out in the wrong order. I'm not mad, just got a very busy mind. But just as real fur can't be activated with sonic technology, a real mammoth doesn't have oil in its ear joints. In fact, it doesn't have "ear joints" at all. And you certainly can't make it do this...'

Just as he'd made the oil in the Zoo's gate hinges explode, the Doctor aimed the sonic screwdriver at the place where the mammoth's ear met its head. A strange high-pitched whirring filled the air. As the machinery inside the mammoth started to vibrate, the mammoth's fur shook, rippling all over its body like a cat under a hairdryer. The whirring changed to a keening screech that increased in intensity the longer the Doctor aimed the sonic screwdriver at the beast.

Then, with a loud thunk, a little hatch sprung open on the side of the mammoth, just below its ear. Inside the white fur, and below the skin, was hidden an intricate machine of shining metal and whirring levers. A delicate spiral of cogs and levers connected each muscle. From a distance it looked like the inside of an expensive watch, or the innermost workings of a town clock. The mechanism was sparkling clean, glinting in the moon light. Where the ear met the head, there was a masterpiece of engineering. Amy could see wires, pistons and sensors, and things she'd never seen in her Technology class in school. The Doctor whistled, as if he couldn't help but admire the boldness of a plan that involved someone disguising alien technology as a mammoth.

With another blast of the sonic screwdriver, the cogs started to rattle, then stopped entirely. A few levers twitched, then there was a loud bang, and they settled down. The Doctor waited and watched.

'I think that's shut it down...' He looked delighted. 'This is so much better than just burgers! It was a disguise all along! How brilliant! Just brilliantly stupid! Imagine the poor creatures that made this. They came to Earth, went to the trouble of disguising their spaceship, but, they got it wrong! It's the twenty-first century, and they built a spy robot pretending to be a mammoth!'

'Says the Time Lord disguised as a geography teacher.'

'Shut up, I look cool – you should pay more attention, Leadworth girl.' The Doctor went up to the shiny hatch. 'Still, the Shadow Proclamation could be tied up for years debating this. Sending a robot spy craft down, pretending to be an extinct animal, no doubt looking for something or other. I guess it was meant to scope out the planet for a suitable invasion... I'm just amazed they got the colour wrong.'

'Do you ever stop talking?' Underneath everything, Amy thought she could hear a *stomp-stomp-stomp*. She was worried by what she'd heard, but couldn't quite trust her ears. 'I don't think it's deactivated...'

Amy felt a tingle run down her spine. She listened again, and was sure she could hear the sound of heavy footsteps, getting louder and louder, building in size and reach.

In the cage next to them, an elephant started to trumpet in panic, bashing the bars of his cage, eager to get away.

'Just listen!' Amy implored. There it was again. Stomp. Stomp. Stomp. Still quiet, but definitely getting closer. 'What could be making that noise?'

she asked. 'Did you say anything about a Trojan horse?'

'No, that would be impossible. There's barely room in there for…' The Doctor looked at the size of mammoth. 'Well, maybe one or two people.'

They both started to back away.

The noise came again. STOMP. STOMP. STOMP.

'But that sounds like hundreds of feet marching,' Amy insisted.

The Doctor nodded grimly. 'Like an army. Could be some kind of TARDIS technology… A different dimension, but I'd have noticed. Maybe it's a temporal gateway, but the readings are wrong…'

Amy looked at the Doctor. 'Doctor, what if they wanted the fur to be wrong? What if they wanted to make it rare so it'd be brought here? What if they wanted to be caught?'

Ever nearer, and even louder – STOMP! STOMP! STOMP!

Then the noise stopped.

It was so quiet Amy was sure she could hear her own heartbeat.

Very, very quietly, the Doctor and Amy moved their heads to listen to the mammoth. There was a sound like a key being turned in a lock.

FATOOM! The entire belly of the mammoth hit the floor.

The Doctor and Amy gazed in wonder. The mammoth had been split neatly in half and now looked like a dismantled toy – normal on top, but all of its lower half descended to the floor. Bright lights blazed out from within the mammoth and, finally, its innards were revealed. The inside of the mammoth looked like a gleaming alien spaceship. The muscle and skin had been no more than a thin shell around a metal body, packed with fantastic-looking alien technology.

'Whoa. What is that?' Amy looked at the Doctor as, with a loud creak, the head of the mammoth turned to face them. 'I thought you said it was turned off.'

The Doctor shrugged. 'Looks like I was wrong.'

'Will it shoot?' Amy asked.

'Don't be ridiculous,' the Doctor replied. 'It's a mammoth, it doesn't have laser guns. It will gore us with those tusks...'

Amy failed to feel reassured.

With a loud hiss, the mammoth's belly was swathed in smoke, and from within the haze came the sound of boots marching, many times louder than before. STOMP! STOMP! STOMP! Hundreds of boots, stamping hard as they marched along the metal insides of the beast.

Above this barbarian sound, they could hear a high-pitched 'Left, right, left, right, left, right'.

As the stomp got louder, the animals of the Zoo were getting restless, uniting in fear, as a mood of chaos spread in the chilly air. The unholy cacophony of bellows, yowls and panicked growls echoed around the enclosures.

Amy instinctively took a step back, freaked by the massed cries of the Zoo animals.

The Doctor took a step forward. 'Now that *is* interesting.' He peered into the hazy light. 'Someone has put an entire army in there. There's something coming out, Amy, down here, look!'

He dived onto his belly, and Amy joined him on the floor. They were now at eye level with the metallic lower half of the beast. As the smoke cleared, they could see that on top of the living muscle was what looked like the deck of an aircraft carrier. It was marked up with arrows, tiny lettering labelled Muster Points and Lift Zones. With a whirring noise, tiny gun turrets rose out of the deck and swivelled to point at the Doctor and Amy.

Everything stopped.

Amy looked to the Doctor. 'Should we, er, be so close to it?'

'Probably not…' the Doctor agreed.

They started to get to their feet, but it was too late.

The mammoth let out a massive blast from its trunk, and the entire Zoo fell silent. It sounded like no animal Amy had ever heard, as if someone had combined the hunting cry of a hungry wolf howl, with the deathly rattle of a cat screech and the murderous growl of a grizzly bear. This was a bloodthirsty call. But it was no animal sound… This was alien.

When it faded, Amy took her hands away from her ears. 'What was that?'

'I think we're about to find out…' the Doctor replied.

Green-tinged energy beams zapped from the bottom of the mammoth to the top, illuminating the inside with a crackly glow. The beams joined together, weaving around each other, until they formed a living, swirling sphere of green energy. Burning like a poisonous star, the plasma whirl of green light grew in strength, becoming brighter and brighter.

Amy shielded her eyes, as it swelled to twice its size and then shrank back down to its burning core. There followed a massive explosion of green energy, zooming out across the Zoo like a shockwave, making the animals ripple as it passed through them. It was a ripple that never lost its power. A wave that kept on crashing. Unstoppable, it spread out from the Zoo and made its way across New York.

At first nothing changed.

'That felt weird,' Amy told the Doctor. 'It was like I was weightless for a second.' She waved her hand in front of her face. 'All my fingers working, and still not webbed. All looking good.'

'Amy, you know we said the Zoo was in the

middle of the city… How accurate do you think that was?'

'It's pretty much the middle of Manhattan, halfway down the island, and right in the centre. Oh…' Amy stopped when she realised what the Doctor was thinking. 'So that green thing… this is probably where they wanted to set it off from?'

The Doctor nodded back towards the belly. 'This wasn't a mistake. This is an invasion.'

The marching noise had stopped. And standing in formation on the deck of the belly was a phalanx of hundreds of tiny, vicious alien soldiers.

Chapter
9

The aliens had heads like angry trolls, all hairy and mean, and wore huge spiked helmets like the Kaiser's army in the First World War. Their short bodies were festooned with weapons: vicious curved swords, stabbing daggers, hand grenades and the most extraordinary guns Amy could ever have imagined.

A high-pitched voice yelled 'Present Arms!' and the massed ranks of aliens raised the guns so they were aiming right at the Doctor and Amy. Their leader marched forward through the rows of alien soldiers, holding himself like a man who knows his rightful place is in command. He carried a baton, and had a magnificently plumed red helmet. As he passed each row, he bellowed at the troops, making them snap into order. They were all clearly terrified of him.

Only one thing stopped Amy from shrinking back with fear. The soldiers were about seven centimetres tall.

'They're like toys!' She burst out laughing. 'How cute.'

She stretched her hand out above the battalion to measure their size. 'Wow! There's a whole army of them! Can I keep them, Doctor? Oh, please say I can? They had the perfect invasion plan, so long as no one stands on them by mistake.'

The first row of soldiers armed their weapons and aimed them at Amy's hand.

The Doctor was very quiet and very serious. He gently moved Amy's hand away, and addressed himself to the figure that was obviously their General. His tiny features were twitching with frustration and rage. Amy thought he looked like Wayne Rooney at his angriest and most stubborn, red faced and blotchy, ready to scream at the world at the least hint of subordination.

'Sorry about her, she's new, well, so to speak. I'm the Doctor, and what *are* you doing here?'

The General turned to his troops and signalled them to lower their weapons. He stepped forward, hit a button on his baton, and rose on a lift, until he was eye to eye with the Doctor. The little alien pointed his baton at the Doctor and scanned his eyes, then turned sharply to Amy and repeated the move.

'You confirm my observations. One humanoid, early stages of evolutionary development. No gills. Limited intellect. And one unidentified species.'

'Time Lord, Oncoming Storm, Defender of Earth, take your pick. But who are you?' the Doctor asked the forceful little alien.

'I am Erik, General of the 99th Vykoid Expeditionary Force. I have at my disposal the might and fury of the Vykoid Army. And you will surrender to me!'

Amy looked at General Erik with curiosity. He had the unconvincing swagger of a new boy on his first day at school. Brash and knowing, yet a look that suggested he'd be only too easy to unsettle.

'Nah,' the Doctor was saying. 'Not surrendering to you in a beast like that. You've come prepared for the wrong century, make that wrong millennia… You're not going to get anywhere if those are your wheels. Now look, not to worry, I can help you get home, but I won't have a war. I forbid it. No one gets hurt today.'

To capture the moment, Amy slid her phone open and snapped a picture on her mobile phone. General Erik's face reddened with rage.

'That's not helping,' the Doctor said to Amy. 'Peace in Our Time wasn't interrupted by passers-by uploading the pictures onto Facebook…'

'Peace in Our Time didn't last long anyway,' Amy pointed out. 'It didn't end up saving any lives.'

General Erik waved his baton angrily. 'You are fools. We will take no lives. Our slaves will work for the glory of the new Vykoid Empire.'

Amy could see the Doctor flinch at the word, his revolve hardening. 'What do you mean – slaves?' he demanded.

With the confidence of the victor, General Erik calmly explained. 'We have a more worthwhile occupation for these New Yorkers. I have observed them today, and they are a weak and unproductive species. The Desiccated mines of Cassetia 2 have been waiting for workers. We hoped to take the famous mighty beasts of Ancient Earth to do the work of millions of Vykoids. But as there are none left, I shall return instead with millions of your well-fed drones.'

The Doctor's face fell. He looked more than a little disgusted. 'Amy, have you heard of the island in the Pacific made up of dried seagull droppings? After hundreds of years it turns into guano and it's mined to be made into explosives.' Amy pulled a face as the Doctor kept on. 'Well the Cassetia asteroids were excreted several millions years ago by a mighty Space-Boar. A race of giant carnivores, they ate only rotting meat from the swamps of Malmatine 5, and grew so huge they evolved into creatures capable of travelling in space. A herd of

Space-Boars ate their way around the universe for 20,000 years before producing the asteroids. Some say it's the worst smell in the entire galaxy. The most concentrated foul stench you can possibly imagine. I've heard terrible stories of the Vykoid slave mines. The smell is so foul, that one whiff can make your hair fall out, and turn your eyes green. The atmosphere of the mines actually prolongs the lives of the slaves. Anyone they take will work for three hundred years or more…'

General Erik's plan seemed insane to Amy. There were millions of people in New York, and there was no way the miniature army could simply kidnap *all* of them. 'Doctor? Can't they, you know, take the animals here?'

'Not exactly fair on the poor animals, is it? But hang on, good point, why can't you take beasts from elsewhere?'

Amy thought she could see General Erik grinning. 'You will be easier to defeat.'

Amy was surprised by his confidence. The Vykoid army had the enchanting freedom of shipwrecked men, with nothing more to lose, and everything to gain. Amy whispered in the Doctor's ear. 'We can stop them, right?'

The Doctor grinned at Amy. 'Oh, yes!' Turning his head away from General Erik, he addressed the neat ranks of soldiers, gazing into their beady little eyes. 'Listen to me, army of Vykoid warriors. Your war is over. Your time has gone. There is not a single person or creature on the planet that you are fit to touch. Return to your planet, and tell everyone you meet that the people of Earth are born free. You got a problem with that? Come see me!'

The Vykoid troops watched the Doctor stony-faced.

'And don't listen to old Sour-Face here,' the Doctor went on, pointing at General Erik. 'Look around you! This is a place of beauty and life. You will not harm anyone. Now, scram, before I have to do something about it.'

General Erik became even more furious. 'I will not be undermined in front of my troops by this lumbering beast. By a pacifist! All my years of training in the Vykoid army have prepared me for moments like this. I have heard the legends of the great Vykoid heroes, and soon it will be my time to join them.' He puffed out his diminutive chest and went on. 'I too will have a statue built for me, in the Hall of Honour on our home planet! Efficiency and punctuality are the backbone of any successful military campaign, and since we seem to have woken up several thousand years too late, I am not about to waste any more time.'

His speech finished, General Erik turned his back on the Doctor, and barked at his men: 'Activate the Temporal Lock!'

The ranks split, and a select group of soldiers

quick-marched back into the mammoth. They obviously hadn't been deterred by the Doctor's speech, and seemed only too keen to follow General Erik's commands.

'Doctor?' Amy raised an eyebrow. 'What's a temporal lock?'

The mammoth was beginning to stir into life once more. Lights were clicking on inside its body, shining out of its eyes and ears. With a grinding noise, the mammoth's trunk was raised into the air, and started to revolve like an aerial.

The Doctor scrambled to his feet and took Amy's hand. 'I think, given the circumstances, it would be a good idea if we *run*!'

Amy couldn't tear her eyes from the Vykoid troops. Everything they did was so regimented and neat. She thought that this might just be the best-organised army she'd ever seen. General Erik was shouting commands and waving his hands around, and the front ranks appeared to be preparing to attack something.

With a sudden feeling of dread, Amy realised who they were getting ready to attack. 'Running… yeah… I'm definitely with you on that.'

But before they could move, the air around them glowed green, just as it had when the circular wave had exploded. Amy could feel every cell in her body vibrate, like she was undergoing her own mini-earthquake. After it had passed through her, she could see the effects travelling over the whole Zoo – the rhinos and elephants shuddering as they shook.

'What was that?' she asked.

The Doctor patted himself up and down. 'I feel... the same as before... but... Oh, Amy, look at that.'

In the few seconds they had looked away, the Vykoid Army had equipped themselves with hundreds of tiny combat vehicles, rather like toy jeeps, and were preparing to move out.

The Doctor stepped closer. 'I thought I told you lot to...'

Something extraordinary was happening. The Vykoids were now moving with impossible speed, like Keystone Cops on fast forward. In the time it took the Doctor to make one step, they had unloaded mini combat helicopters, tanks and troop transporters. There was even a mobile kitchen set up, serving out soup to the troops.

'How did they do that?' Amy asked.

By the time she'd finished the question, the Vykoid army had put wheels on the base of the air deck in the mammoth's belly and had loaded it up to depart.

Amy moved quickly, and flung herself at the army, determined to stop them throwing themselves at New York. As much for their sake as hers. She didn't want a new species to be slaughtered, just by misjudging their sense of scale.

But as she lunged, Amy felt hundreds of pinpricks on her ankles. The Vykoid troops were scampering up her legs, so quickly she could barely make them out. These were specialist climbing Vykoids, equipped with ropes, carabiners and the like. She may have imagined it, but Amy was sure they stopped for a tea break on her kneecap, before continuing their climb.

Within seconds, Amy had been pulled to the ground, every bit of her tied and secured. General Erik marched onto her face and peered into her large eyes. To him, she must have seemed like some wondrous deep-sea creature, all plate-sized eyes, enormous limbs and improbable physics.

This close to him, Amy could see the Vykoid's features properly for the first time. His skin was tough, like leather left out too long in the elements, and his eyes were mean and dark. The spirit of conquest was strong in him, and Amy felt rebellion rise in her heart – she would not be bested by him.

General Erik didn't talk, he boomed. 'Do you accept our victory?'

'No!' Amy bellowed back. Her breath was so strong General Erik was almost rocked off his feet.

'Analyse her!' he snapped, and in a flash he was replaced with dozens of white-coated Vykoids. Scientist Vykoids, Amy thought, trying to clear her head of the notion that she could feed the Vykoid army for a millennium, should they decide to eat her. Or, even worse, they could make their next vehicle inside her... Where was the Doctor when she needed him?

She tried to turn her head but was rewarded with a sharp jab in her ear, and an outraged squeaking from below. 'Sorry!' she called out. 'I can't see you back there, don't have eyes in the back of my head.'

As one, the Vykoid scientists started lifting her hair and examining her scalp for hidden eyes.

Then, as rapidly as they'd arrived, the Vykoids had gone. Not a squeak to be heard. And it had got dark. Amy realised she had been unconscious – she must have been out for hours.

She lifted her hand and found it was no longer restrained. Luckily, the Zoo was well lit, so she could see her watch. She was amazed to see that it was close to midnight. She also saw that her hand had been stamped in bold red ink: 'Not Suitable.'

Amy guessed that this was a good thing. The entire Vykoid army had shipped on out. But, oh, this was much, much worse than she'd thought. They had left her behind, but they had taken the Doctor with them. She was on her own in New York. And the Army of the Vykoids was marching to take Manhattan.

Chapter
10

Around her, the animals had gone back to their night-time activities – meerkats chittering to themselves and giraffes sleeping quietly.

'Doctor!' she shouted into the Zoo, but there was no reply. She kept thinking his tousled head might emerge, grinning like it was all part of his plan, but it looked like he was really gone. This was hopeless. Amy was going to have to stop the Vykoids alone.

'OK, don't panic,' she told herself. 'Just think – what would the Doctor do? First off, no talking to yourself, definitely a bad thing…'

She was alone, in a locked cage in a zoo, while an army of tiny soldiers had been let loose in New York. She had no idea what they wanted, or how she was going to find the Doctor.

'Come on, come on,' she thought. 'Not done yet. Assets, Assets! OK, no Doctor, no sonic screwdriver, no ray gun... and still talking to myself.'

Amy put her hand into her pocket, and was delighted to find the psychic paper. 'Ha! Just what I need.'

As confident as Amy liked to pretend to be in front of the Doctor, she had rarely been alone in a foreign city before, let alone one being invaded by diminutive aliens. She told herself she just had to focus on finding the Doctor. Amy wasn't one for fainting or calling out for help.

So, to her great surprise, Amy found herself searching for tracks in the sawdust and hay of the Zoo, peering into the gloom of the night. Skirting the now quiet and still mammoth, she saw neat rows of tiny footprints and tyre tracks from the miniature jeeps. And alongside was a larger dragging mark, which could only be the Doctor.

Amy fought to keep down her sense of panic. The Doctor had been kidnapped by a tiny alien race, but he was bound to be all right. He'd been through far worse, and even if he was in trouble, he'd be fine as soon as she found him.

Following the Vykoid trail was tricky. They'd darted through tiny openings, and Amy found herself squeezing through gaps, and heading over large objects. At one fence, she was impressed to see that the Vykoids had made time to construct a ramp up and down either side so they could march straight over the top, dragging the Doctor behind. Like a column of ants, they'd taken their prey and had headed single-mindedly out of the Zoo.

The trail led Amy out onto Fifth Avenue. Looking up for a moment, Amy gazed in wonder at the New York skyline, gleaming in the night sky. If anything, it looked bigger at night. A vast tribute to human might, with office lights shining far brighter than the stars and galaxies above. It was true what they said: bright lights, big city.

But as she marvelled at Fifth Avenue, Amy realised she had lost any way of tracking the Vykoids. The hard tarmac showed no traces of the tiny army, and even the Doctor's drag marks were impossible to see. Amy hadn't imagined she'd ever yearn to have a husky as a faithful companion, but short of finding a big sign saying 'Doctor this way', she was stumped… She couldn't even go back to the TARDIS, as the Doctor had hidden it and she had no idea of how to get it back.

Amy wasn't intimidated by what was ahead. She had always made the most of where she was and – whether it was Leadworth or New York – she wasn't about to let herself flounder. Smiling, she thought to herself of the new gang she'd form. The Pond Gang.

With this in mind, Amy was delighted to get back to their stolen squad car – and to see a familiar figure silhouetted at the wheel of another police patrol car across the road from her.

Oscar seemed to have nodded off to sleep, but Amy's squeal of delight woke him up.

'Hey!' Amy called through the car window. 'A sexy man in uniform waiting to look after me. You don't know it yet, but you are just what I wanted to find.'

Stepping out of his car, Oscar looked Amy up and down. 'What's that on your clothes?' he asked, pointing at the elephant dung. 'Smells like—'

'Shut up!' Amy cut him off. 'This is an emergency. A big one. Just here. Me, in fact. I need your help.' Amy winked at Oscar. 'Work with me, I'll see if I can put a good word in. Who knows, could be a promotion in this for you.'

Oscar didn't look that impressed by Amy's offer, but she pressed on. 'It's good to see you again, Oscar. I thought I'd have to ring 999 or something, sorry, should be 911 shouldn't it. But no – here you are already! That's what I call community policing.'

Oscar seemed perturbed by her attitude, and Amy decided to try a different approach. She hadn't watched all of *Glee* without learning a bit about American culture. 'My friend is in great danger, and I need you to help me find him.' She thought she should lay it on a bit thicker for his sentimental American side and continued: 'Of course, thing is, I'm at a point in my life now where I have some big decisions to make, and its getting kind of tough but I'm gonna pull through it all, thing is, I need your help, tonight, and I will be grateful for ever.' It seemed to be working. At least, Oscar was not actually disagreeing with her. 'Oh, and another thing – we're going to need a dog. You can manage that can't you?'

Amy smiled. She was getting the hang of this. Of all the things she'd thought New York had to offer, chatting up hot cops was definitely an added bonus. And here she was, assembling a crack team to save New York. Back home, Rory wouldn't even trust her to make a cup of tea, let alone choose the button that might save the world. Now, she was like *The A-Team* meets *Cagney and Lacey*. Since meeting the Doctor she'd had the chance to do so much more, and be better then she'd ever imagined. Now she was ready to go solo.

Oscar had retreated back into his squad car, having a long conversation with someone on his phone. He hadn't told Amy who he was calling, but from the sound of it, he was pretty scared of them.

As he ended the call, Amy leant in the window, and smiled as nicely as she could. 'So have we got a pooch?'

Oscar nodded, with a pained expression that he was doing his best to hide. 'The tracker dog is on its way.'

*

Back in her office, Commander Strebbins had called in all the officers she had at her disposal, and had placed the city on a Level One alert. She had no intelligence to back this up, but knew in her gut that she needed to get the pieces in place. She was more than happy to let Oscar have whatever resources he needed as long as he was sticking with the enigmatic Amy Pond.

Her records showed that Amy was nothing more than a kissogram from a small town in England. She had no connections to UNIT and there were no records of her working with the Doctor, yet she had thrown herself into the action at the Museum like a seasoned professional. She was definitely hiding something, and Strebbins suspected it would lead to the heart of the matter.

Amy was impressed with the speed at which Oscar had been able to summon help. As she waited on the pavement, he was talking earnestly to another police officer, who was mid-handover of an excitable Alsatian.

As Oscar signed some papers, Amy gazed again at the New York skyline, glowing brightly in the night sky. This was a place where so many people had come to find their dreams and start their lives all over again. Perhaps it was true, and if Amy could make it here, she'd be able to make it anywhere. Oscar seemed a good start for the Pond Gang, if a bit quiet. He had a disconcerting habit of noting down everything Amy said, but as long as he was on her side she didn't really mind.

She'd thought of recruiting the new officer who had turned up, but he'd been decidedly grumpy, and she could do without that. Amy heard the dog van's engines start up, and pull off to reveal Oscar, fully kitted up, and a bouncy Alsatian by his side. Her team was in place. She smiled, and said out loud, 'Bring it on, New York!'

Then, one by one, the skyscrapers' lights started to go out.

First the Empire State Building changed from a beacon of light to a mere silhouette, then the Bank of Manhattan became a slab of black granite. New York was losing power and flickering like cameras at a concert, the entire skyline changed to black.

Amy stared up Fifth Avenue as a wave of Upper West Side's grand buildings all receded into darkness. The streetlamps that marked out the grids of the city so neatly lost their sodium glow and, block by block, New York became as dark as the heart of the rainforest…

Amy looked around her in horror. New York had been blackened by an accumulation of night. She wasn't scared of the dark, but dark in a city was a different kind of feeling. The buildings around her now looked like tombstones, mere ghosts of skyscrapers, casting dark blots and angles against the sky. Manhattan felt smaller, and more dangerous. Only the island of Manhattan had lost power, and the orange spill of Queens and New Jersey marked the edge of the blackout zone. But rather than reassure Amy, it made the city feel even darker, totally enclosed.

All around her, office buildings were emptying early for the night. People were starting to pile out onto the streets, laughing and cheering; grinning late-shift workers, delighted to be released from a night of hard work stuck to their computers. She was sure she could see a firework going off above Harlem. New Yorkers loved a party, and this looked like it was going to make Saturday night a whole lot more fun.

Wandering near her, a girl was struggling with her phone.

'Hello? Dan? Are you there? I don't know how I'm going to get home.'

Amy called out to Oscar. 'Check your phone.'

He gave the answer she was expecting: 'It isn't working.'

As Amy listened, she heard a kind of quiet that hadn't reached the city in decades. Nothing was working. Bars were shutting their doors, restaurant kitchens were closing, the Metro lines were down, as all the things the city relied on had simply stopped.

When she was a child back in Scotland, they'd sometimes had blackouts that lasted for hours –

technology briefly beaten back by snow, or floods, or just by a car hitting a pylon. But there were twelve million people here, and Amy knew the lights weren't going to snap on any time soon like they had in Inverness.

Amy wanted to stop everyone walking past and shepherd them inside. This wasn't a temporary fault or an excuse for a short-lived party in the dark. The Vykoid Army was behind this and, unless Amy could find the Doctor and stop them, light wasn't going to return to New York.

She was baffled by how powerful the pint-sized aliens were. They were a strange and terrifying kind of army. They operated anonymously under the shadow of darkness, and with a motive so clear and so brutal it was difficult to do anything but plunge into conflict with them. A battle Amy desperately wanted to avoid.

If only she could find the Doctor.

Chapter
11

Oscar had already raced back to his car and pulled out his radio to call in to the station. Amy hurried over, leant in and switched it off.

'Hey!' Oscar protested.

Amy simply smiled at him. 'You don't need that thing any more. I'll give you all the commands you'll need. So – down to business. I've lost my friend, and I need you to help me find him. So get Fido over here, and let's go!'

'Lady, are you seriously telling me that in the middle of the biggest blackout since 1922, you expect me to help *you*?'

Amy smiled. 'Don't take it so hard. You may have won the War of Independence, but right now you can consider yourself my colonial conquest...'

Oscar considered for a moment, then nodded in agreement.

Amy beamed at him 'Good! Let's go to work then, partner.' She cheerily took the car keys out of the ignition and called to the dog. 'Over here, Fido!'

Oscar's sniffer dog leapt up at her, excited to be on a case after hours dozing on the station floor. Amy pulled a bow tie from her pocket and dangled it in front of the dog. 'This is one of his most colourful,' she confided. 'I've confiscated it, in case he ever decides to wear it…'

The dog was acting strangely, not used to the smell of a Time Lord.

'Come on,' Amy went on. 'There's a good dog. Eurgh, this actually has one of his hairs on it,' Amy pulled away a long strand of hair, adding, 'He is such a girl.'

Oscar was watching Amy with a weary look on his face. He clapped his hands, and the dog ran to his feet. 'His name is Bismarck. And he'll do as I say…' Another clap of his hands had Bismarck tracing the ground for a scent, dashing to and fro in ten-metre bursts, covering the area methodically.

'My friend was on the pavement there.' Amy pointed, but Oscar looked confused. 'Oh, OK, if it makes you happy, on the *sidewalk*. Honestly, it's not like you've got a mainwalk, is it?'

Oscar opened his mouth to answer, but then Bismarck gave a businesslike bark and started to hare along the sidewalk towards downtown New York.

Amy turned to Oscar, surprised. 'I thought he might have been taken to Central Park or something. Wouldn't someone have noticed a man being dragged along the street?'

This was something Oscar did understand. 'You see all sorts in New York, ma'am. Takes a lot to stop traffic.'

As they followed Bismarck, Oscar asked: 'So, tell me about this guy we're trying to find.'

'The Doctor?' Amy paused. There was something about Oscar that made her want to tell him everything. 'He's the most amazing man you'll ever meet, Oscar. So wonderful, and so kind, and able to do the most incredible things. He's shown me places I didn't know existed, and made me realise I can do things I never expected. But most of all, he'll walk across the galaxies to stop a single innocent life being lost. He's the man I've been waiting for almost my whole life, and now I've found him, it's even better than I expected.'

From his expression, Oscar clearly thought Amy was in love with the Doctor. She quickly decided to tone down the limitless appreciation.

'He's also a complete buffoon, with a silly fringe, and bandy legs, and the most bizarre way of talking. But if he was here, Oscar, he'd have the lights back on again in a second.'

Amy realised Oscar was now trying to work out exactly how mad she was. She smiled at her tame New York cop. 'Don't think so hard, Oscar. Tomorrow you may never see me again. This is the life, eh? On the trail of a mystery man with a dog at midnight. Plus you get a hot companion for your evening's work…'

Oscar blushed.

'No need to be shy, Oscar,' Amy continued. 'I might need a cocktail later…'

The police dog led them down Fifth Avenue, past the Metro station, and towards the looming arch of the Grand Army Plaza Memorial, more sombre than ever in the dark.

'Right, it's my turn now,' Amy said, eager to reverse the stakes with Oscar. 'So what got you into this? Was it *Starsky and Hutch* or *The Sopranos*?' Oscar didn't know what to say. 'Or maybe *The A-Team*? Come on, you can tell me, I know what it's all about. A great battle of good versus evil, you on the side of good, plus you get to wear a sexy uniform.'

'My dad was a cop,' Oscar mumbled.

Amy nodded. 'Good reason. Better than my reason for joining the police.'

'Why?' Oscar asked curiously.

'The Chief of Police in New Scotland Yard made a deal: either turn cop, or do a ten-year stretch…'

'No way!' Oscar said, wide-eyed with astonishment.

'Course not, dumbo!' Amy laughed. 'Imagine me, in stripy prisoner clothes! I am going to have so much fun winding you up. We'll be like the new Bonnie and Clyde, except, of course, we'll be good guys.'

Amy's laughter was interrupted by a sudden crash. Far up the street, towards Central Park, she could see people running into the middle of the street. A massive plate glass window had smashed into tiny fragments, showering shards on the pavement. Amy and Oscar stared up the road, Bismarck growling at the unseen aggressor.

There was a second crash, and another window fell into little pieces. This time the building was nearer to them.

'What's happening?' Oscar asked

Before Amy could answer, they saw a brick fly through the windscreen of the stolen squad car. Its alarm made a weak bleat, like a newborn lamb. Drained of power, like everything else in the city it soon fell silent.

'I told the Doctor we shouldn't have taken the car,' Amy told Oscar. 'That's gonna take some explaining.'

'Amy,' Oscar was agitated. 'That brick. No one threw it. I was watching... How'd it fly through the air by itself?'

Another crash echoed through the night.

The lamp-post above their heads shattered.

They ducked as the glass fell, then leapt clear as the lamp-post itself fell and slammed into the ground between them.

Amy looked Oscar in the eye. 'I don't really know. I normally get to ask questions like that.'

With a series of ear-splitting roars, the glass windows of the Trump Tower above them began to crack, lines breaking across it, as if hundreds of abseiling window cleaners were having a mad moment of rebellion and cracking each pane with the heels of their boots.

'But,' Amy continued, 'there's something you probably need to know.'

Behind them, Central Park's ducks rose up from the lake in terror – the water stirred to a frenzy by some unknown force. The lake settled again, but a fearsome whirlpool at its heart began to spread its vortices across the lake. The water was being drained away, as if someone had pulled a plug.

Amy had never seen such madness. She stood in the middle of Fifth Avenue and watched as every lamp-post in sight was torn from its footings and thrown into the road. Drinkers chucked out of the bars were having the beer bottles torn from their hands.

Around them the air was filled with a vicious clanging of metal being bent out of shape. In front of them, the façades of the buildings were being pitted with tiny holes.

Something was descending down Fifth Avenue with the force and fury of an army of the undead.

'Have you noticed?' Oscar asked. 'Everything is being smashed in a line.'

Sure enough, the chaos appeared to be moving along the street, people running in front of the mayhem, desperate to avoid the flying debris in the air.

'Yep. And the exciting thing is it's heading this way.' Amy came to a halt in the midst of the debris. 'But we're not moving.'

'What?' asked Oscar incredulously.

'Look at it. They're sweeping everyone off the streets. Someone wants us to move, Oscar. And I'm not feeling very cooperative today.'

Amy knew she was right. First the Vykoids had killed the power, and now they were sweeping the streets clear of people. If the same thing was happening across the city, then everyone on the streets was being herded downtown. Amy didn't want to tell Oscar what was going to happen to people when they got there.

'They're going to have to do more than this to move us out of the way,' she said.

As the lamp-posts crashed down, Amy pulled Oscar close to her, and the wave of mayhem moved past them.

'Told you it would be OK.' Amy grinned from ear to ear.

Oscar was looking at her with a serious expression on his face. 'You said "they". I just reckoned New York had been hit by freak weather conditions. What do you mean "they"?'

Amy hesitated. 'Oscar, there's no easy way to tell you this. But I knew we wouldn't get hurt. This isn't an accident. It's a plan. Breaking glass, tearing down lamp-posts. It's scary, but look, no one's been hurt. Not many people could do that. And I've seen something today that you're going to find hard to believe. So bite your lip, and just keep thinking of when you were young and saw things that couldn't be true, but they turned out to be the real thing.'

Oscar nodded, keen to hear anything that might still the panic that was rising in him.

Amy continued. 'The things doing this aren't people. They're aliens. They're an alien army. Something that's been hidden on Earth for so long it was forgotten. Now they're awake, and they want New York. There was a lot more than we thought inside that mammoth, and it's got out.'

'I don't get you,' Oscar said, thinking that maybe she was a nutter after all.

'Have you got binoculars?' Amy asked.

'What?'

'Just… Binoculars. Please.'

Oscar went through his pockets, pulling out a pair. Amy looked down the street until she spotted a lamp-post that was still standing. She squinted at the ground around it, then gave a short cry of triumph.

'Yes! That one, there. Focus on that one, that's right – you'll need to be quick. Right at the base of the post.'

Oscar focused the binoculars on the lamp-post, then gasped with astonishment as he saw a team of ten tiny aliens cutting into its base with a minuscule circular saw, while others tied tiny wires around the pole.

Without binoculars, Amy could barely make out what was happening. It felt like she was watching time-lapse photography, the tiny Vykoids were moving so fast. In only a few seconds, they'd cut away a chunk of metal at the base, and pulled the pole onto the ground.

'That's not possible!' Oscar exclaimed. 'Have you put something in my drink?'

Amy put her hands on his shoulders. 'I know this is a bit crazy, your head is probably spinning like you've had too much coffee, and part of you wants to sit down and give up. But you're not going to. You've been sent to follow me 'cos you're the best they've got.'

'How did you know that?' Oscar demanded.

Amy smiled. 'Oscar, everyone in New York could tell you were waiting for me.' She continued. 'While we're together, we're safe. We can beat these things.'

Oscar frowned. 'I'll get in touch with Commander Strebbins, and we'll get all the units we need. We have weapons so smart, the tech guys have probably got something perfect for blasting tiny people into even tinier pieces.'

Amy put her hand on his mouth. 'Haven't you been listening to me? We do this without guns, without violence. Today, no one's going to get hurt. Those are the things that have my friend, and the Doctor is the only person who can stop them. If we can get him back he'll know exactly what to do.'

Oscar was looking at Amy in obvious confusion. 'How can you be so calm about this? This is crazy. It's like Jim Henson's workshop has come to life out there!'

Amy could tell how stressed he was, how much he wanted to fall back on what he'd normally do – pull a gun and tell the criminals to stand down. 'I need you at your best, Oscar. Just trust me.' She gave him a hug.

'We're gonna need more troops for this,' he insisted. 'We can't handle this alone…'

Amy sighed. 'I bet you were scared of noises in the night when you were young.'

Oscar nodded.

'And then you found out it was just the wind blowing,' Amy said, 'and you knew it was going to be OK?'

Oscar nodded again.

Amy smiled. 'Good, then think of them like they're the wind. You can't shoot it, but you can shut it out.'

Oscar still wasn't convinced. 'I just can't believe what I saw. I mean, where are they all gone?'

It was true that the Vykoids had moved on, but Amy couldn't afford to lose her only ally for lack of proof.

'Think for a minute,' she said. 'That's all I'm asking, just think. If they aren't real, then what else do you know that could do all these things?'

Oscar didn't have an answer.

'Maybe you're right, Oscar,' Amy told him, 'and there's no life outside Manhattan, and there's no pride except being NYPD for life. But I've seen more of the universe in the last few days than you can imagine. Sometimes it's the most exhilarating feeling, like riding an amazing rollercoaster through the stars. But there are things out there that are so dark and so tortured they want to conquer and capture everything they meet. The mammoth wasn't a miracle, Oscar. It came back to life because it had thousands of aliens inside it. That's what's causing the chaos on the street.'

Oscar gaped.

'Yeah, it's not like alien attacks in the movies. This one is practically invisible, and sudden, and unless we stop them, they'll get under every bed in New York. You have to believe me, Oscar. You can't fight them like normal criminals. They aren't even a normal army. We need to be smarter than them. Better than them.'

Amy held up her phone so that Oscar could see the screen. 'Here, I think you're ready for the close-up view.' The picture Amy had taken showed Erik the Vykoid squinting angrily at the Doctor, waving his baton in indignation.

'That's them?' Oscar asked incredulously. 'You've met them?'

Amy smiled. She'd got him. 'Yeah, get used to it. Now, you on my side or theirs? Mine, yeah? Thought so! Come on – let's take this together, but we'll do it my way...'

Chapter
12

New York was descending into a night of terror. But one person in the city felt like her hour had come. In a darkened NYPD office, Commander Strebbins was yelling at her colleagues.

'What do you mean radio signals are down?' She slammed her useless phone handset down into its cradle and walked up to her window.

Outside the city was dark and vulnerable. The ill-lit streets below were easy targets for... *something*. This was exactly why she had been put in place. Commander Strebbins knew that her first priority was to protect the banks, shops and private properties. Already there had been reports of looting from downtown department stores. But, an instinct honed through years of police work was tingling.

She suspected that this was the start of something much bigger. And Jackie Strebbins wasn't about to be caught on the hop.

Striding out into the main office, she collared the nearest cop. 'Raise us to Level Three, but I want to hold back on the main units. Don't commit the elite armed police to any crime scene unless you have express orders from me.'

Gathering his courage, the young cop asked, 'How should I get the message out, ma'am?'

Strebbins didn't miss a beat. 'Better start running.'

She didn't like to admit it, but the business with the mammoth had unsettled her. She wasn't one for superstition, but she took anything out of the ordinary as a sign of danger. The UNIT involvement made her uncomfortable. She liked to think she could deal with anything her own way, not rely on someone who came and went when he pleased, and didn't report to anyone.

Maybe the mammoth was just a distraction, and the Doctor had been and gone. But she couldn't shake the feeling that in some other part of town people were getting ready to harm the city she loved. Commander Strebbins was about to make one of the most important calls of her career but, like many such moments, it seemed to her to be the only natural choice she could make.

Strebbins called a cadet over. 'Run to the Mayor's

office, and give him the following message.'

The cadet scrambled for his pad.

'Under protocol 578, I am initiating a period of intense policing under the Night Storm strategy,' Strebbins said rapidly. 'In short, I'm closing down the streets. He better tell the President that there'll be pictures of tanks on Broadway in the papers tomorrow. He'll give you a list of objections. Listen carefully to him, write down everything he says, then throw it in the garbage on the way out.'

Strebbins realised that the cadet was still taking notes.

'You do understand that the last things I said weren't part of the message?'

The cadet blushed and hastily scribbled out the last few lines.

'Then,' Strebbins continued, 'after he's objected for five minutes exactly, give him this next message: "As far as I'm concerned, there is no other course of action open to us." Is that understood?' Strebbins paused. She felt a bit like an old-style general dictating orders like this. And she had to admit she liked it.

'Yes, ma'am,' the cadet replied.

'Good.' Strebbins knew it wasn't going to be easy. She'd be explaining her decision for a long time to come. Yet, as she looked out of her window at the city below, she knew it was a place worth saving. Some people would squawk away, attempting to deny the facts of a situation, or pretend it was about something else entirely. But Strebbins knew what was needed was control. She needed to get the city running again, and nothing and no one was going to stop her.

Amy and Oscar chased after Bismarck the tracker dog, as he led them down Fifth Avenue. As they reached the Arch, Bismarck skidded to a halt and started to growl at something.

Amy could immediately tell that something was very wrong. The debris around this crossroads was worse than the other streets, with three of the roads blocked. Yet one roadway had been left clear. It was far too much of a coincidence for this not to be a trap.

Almost on cue, six blacked-out vehicles screeched up the road and swung into the crossroads. The police vans had blockaded the only passable road, and police officers piled out of the vans. In their full riot gear, they looked like modern-day gladiators, advancing their line towards the scene of the most debris.

One of the police officers lifted his visor and shouted to the street, 'This is now a police-controlled area. Make your way to your homes. The streets are now under police control.'

As they moved down the street, the officers started to wince. The first six riot police suddenly found that their shields had been replaced with an umbrella, a body-board, a poster of President Obama, a baseball glove, and a traffic cone.

They stared in disbelief, raising their guns, only to see those guns taken from their hands. The soldiers squinted in disbelief. On the ground, waving the guns around were groups of red-faced, angry trolls.

Now unarmed, the riot police clung together, watching with horror as their rifles danced around on the floor, being controlled by miniature soldiers.

Amy could see the Vykoids were laughing, and one of them was firing stones from a catapult at incredible speed. Barely bigger than gravel, the stones stung the faces and hands of the troops. Every time they tried to move, more of their riot gear was taken from them.

Amy gestured for Oscar to duck out of sight behind a tree. 'Vykoids…' she whispered. 'There's an army of them out there.'

Oscar's jaw was set. 'Are they gonna shoot?'

Amy shook her head. 'They don't want to kill anyone. But they're going to do something far worse. We've got to stop them.'

Oscar stood bolt upright. 'I'll go tell the riot squad about them!'

Amy yanked him back by his belt. 'No! I meant we've got to stop the police. You've got to listen to me. We can't just charge in there, they can do amazing things to you, I haven't time to explain. Just believe me.'

Oscar was obviously torn. Amy could sympathise – his colleagues were under siege and he wasn't about to stand by and watch them be humiliated. Before Amy could say anything more, Oscar stepped out into the crossroads.

'Whoever you are,' Oscar called out, 'I don't care if we can't see you, I'm here now, and as long as you can see me, you better bet, you're not getting nothing from the city. Do you hear me? I said: *Do you hear me?*'

Buoyed by his upbeat voice, the struggling officers shrugged off their unseen attackers, and gave Oscar a tiny cheer. Amy wondered if she'd been wrong. Perhaps this was Oscar's chance to become a hero after all.

But then the square filled with what only Amy could make out to be the sound of hundreds of mini soldiers laughing. They'd not been put off by Oscar's speech – they found it hilarious.

Amy watched in horror as she saw all the Vykoid troops turn away from the quaking riot police to descend on Oscar. Seeing them advance, Oscar put his hand up to signal a halt. His jaw dropped in amazement – his black NYPD gloves had been replaced with pink lacy ladies gloves, sparkling with Swarsovski crystals.

'What?' As Oscar brought his hands together to

take off the gloves, his baseball cap was suddenly swapped for a pink tiara. He tried to draw his baton, but pulled out a fairy wand. Its tiny bells tinkled as, unable to stop his movement, he waved the wand at the watching soldiers.

The Vykoid troops were doubled up with laughter. It was as if they'd never seen anything as funny as Oscar trying to take them all on.

With increasing horror, Amy realised that, since they moved at lightning speed, Oscar would seem to be moving slower than a tortoise in treacle to the Vykoids. Each of his gestures would take up several minutes of time as the Vykoids experienced it. In the time it would take Oscar to click his fingers, Amy thought, the Vykoids could easily run up and down his body and do whatever they wanted.

As if to confirm the theory, two marker-pen-wielding Vykoids spent a few seconds of Oscar's time drawing a pair of comedy glasses round his eyes and a fake moustache that curled out from under his nose right up his cheeks.

'Stop it now!' Oscar yelled. 'I'm an officer of the New York Police Department, and I will not be played with!'

Unfortunately for Oscar, his authority was undermined by the Vykoids stealing his trousers. Oscar stood in the middle of New York, in his spotty boxers, pink lace gloves and pink tiara, and listened to the sound of tiny aliens laughing. Amy's hand went to her mouth as she struggled not to laugh herself.

'Not funny,' she muttered. '*So* not funny.'

Despite the circumstances, Oscar seemed determined not to beat a retreat. He went for his gun, and this time he seemed to have got the better of the speedy tyrants. He took aim at the Vykoid troops.

'Halt! Be aware that I will shoot. As a real and present danger to the safety of New York, I am arresting you...'

Oscar tailed off. The Vykoids were still laughing at him. One of them put a hand up and, speaking very slowly, asked Oscar, 'Can I have a drink, officer?'

They all burst out laughing again, harder than ever. Oscar stared at his hand in shock. While he'd been talking, they'd replaced his gun with a water pistol.

He fired anyway. In the same instant, a police riot shield appeared between him and the Vykoids, and the water splashed back in his own face.

'I will not surrender to you!' Oscar fumed, as a short miniskirt appeared around his legs.

Amy watched in frustration. She wished he'd listened to her, instead of playing the hero. She couldn't let herself be captured, and was helpless on the sidelines as the Vykoids moved in on Oscar.

'Stay behind the line!' Oscar shouted.

The Vykoids didn't listen. As they spread around him, Oscar turned in a circle, trying to keep his eyes locked on the creatures. Like hummingbirds' wings, they became blurs of movement on the ground, zooming around Oscar's ankles.

'I said stop!'

It was too late. A cord tightened around Oscar's ankles.

'Focus, Oscar!' Amy shouted. She had an idea, but he'd have to be quick. 'Stand on one leg, and move the other round as fast as you can!'

Oscar probably didn't have a clue what Amy was trying to do, but he kicked his left leg high in the air, and waggled it as fast as he could.

'As high up as you can get it,' Amy yelled.

With obvious difficulty, Oscar pulled his leg right up into the air.

Amy's hope was that, in Vykoid time, Oscar now presented them with a technical challenge. They needed to tie his legs together to trip him up or secure him, but the left leg was now too far away for an easy fit. Undeterred, the Vykoids continued to methodically secure their ropes to his right leg, and sent a second team to attach the cords to his left leg, far away, but moving very slowly towards them.

'Now! Swap over, and *kick*!' Amy screamed, talking as fast as she could, desperate to avoid the Vykoids hearing her plan before Oscar.

Some of the Vykoids on the right leg realised

what was happening and started to scarper, but Oscar kicked out, ripping all the ropes from the Vykoids hands and sending a few stragglers flying off into the air.

'Somersault!' Amy commanded.

Oscar froze.

Amy shouted again. 'Forward roll, then.'

Oscar did as he was told and, moving forward like a human woodlouse, he reached Amy. It seemed he was too awkward and too mobile a shape for the Vykoids to have any way of holding him, and the Vykoids signalled a retreat. There were more and easier targets than Oscar, no matter how much fun he was to tease.

'I'd lend you some of my clothes, Oscar,' Amy said, 'but I'm not sure I'd wear a skirt that short.'

Oscar hugged her with relief. 'How did you do that?' he asked.

Amy shrugged. 'I guess I pick things up being around the Doctor. Also,' she said with a smile, 'you weren't getting anywhere by yourself, so I thought I should chip in.'

Oscar's face fell as he looked across the square. While they'd been occupied, the Vykoids had moved in on the riot police. There was not a single NYPD officer left on the crossroads.

'They'll be OK, Oscar,' Amy reassured him. 'The Vykoids don't want to hurt them.'

Amy didn't tell Oscar that they were going

to be taken to an alien planet to mine Space-Boar droppings. She didn't want him doing anything stupid. Again. She told him to go and wait in one of the empty police trucks.

With the scene now clear, Amy walked to the middle of the crossroads and picked up the torch and truncheon the Vykoids had taken from Oscar. Her heart skipped a beat when she saw Oscar's gun lying on the ground. She picked it up, surprised by how heavy and cold it felt. She knew the Doctor wouldn't want her to use it, and she knew in her heart that he was right. But all the other police officers had been taken. Commander Strebbins's crack troops had disappeared, leaving their high-tech vehicles and weapons idling uselessly on the tarmac.

Amy had to admit that the Vykoids had been true to their word. In everything she'd seen, not a soul had been seriously harmed. Teased, yes. Beaten up, a little bit. Kidnapped, and taken as slaves, certainly. But the Vykoids weren't murderers.

This left Amy with a dilemma. She was standing at a crossroads in New York with a gun in her hand. She couldn't just leave it there for anyone to find, and she didn't want to give it back to Oscar…

She walked over to Oscar, who had wrapped himself in a blanket, hiding his legs from the world. The pink gloves and tiara were on the passenger seat of the troopers' vehicle.

'Why did you get rid of those?' Amy teased him. 'It was a good look.'

Oscar smiled. 'I can't thank you enough.'

He was going to go on, but Amy interrupted. 'First thing, you're not having this back.' She popped the chamber out of the gun and emptied the bullets into her hand. She wandered over to a drain cover, intent on dropping the bullets down into the dark.

As she reached into her pocket, her fingers touched the psychic paper. On an instinct, she took it out – and saw a message:

Oi! I'm down here!

Amy's heart leapt with joy. It was the Doctor. The writing on the psychic paper was faint, but then it clearly changed:

I'm below you!

Amy looked from side to side. All she could see were grand department stores, interrupting a steady line of doughnut shops and takeaway coffee stands. A gush of hot air disturbed the ever-present pigeons and they fluttered into the dark sky.

'What's down there?' Amy asked, pointing to vents in the pavement.

Oscar shrugged. 'The Subway. There'll be people trapped down there…'

'That's it!' Amy thought. 'The Vykoids have taken the Doctor underground…' She turned back to Oscar. 'Why do you have a Green Globe to show it's a subway?' she protested. 'Couldn't it just say

"SUBWAY" in big letters?'

Leaving Oscar on the sidewalk, she rushed to the entrance. 'And don't you start asking me to buy a ticket, I am so jumping the barriers.'

Oscar shouted out after her. 'I'd better come with you. It isn't safe at this time of night.'

Amy held up her hand to stop him, and said firmly. 'I'll be fine by myself. It's not the crazy New Yorkers on the Subway I'm worried about right now. Thanks for the help.'

Oscar looked embarrassed. Not only had he had his face drawn all over by tiny aliens from another planet, but now even girls in peril were refusing his help.

Amy smiled. 'Ahem, whole city in danger. You're the only cop to have avoided being captured. I think they're going to need you up here, don't you?' Oscar was wavering, so she ploughed on. '*I* need you up top. Whatever Strebbins is planning, you need to stop it. The more men she sends out, the more people she's giving to the Vykoids.'

Oscar still hesitated, and Amy felt touched by his old-fashioned chivalry.

'C'mere,' she gestured to him. 'You've been brilliant. Just don't think of me as an ordinary girl and that'll put your mind at rest. Thanks for your help.'

Amy planted a big kiss on his cheek. He blushed, and Amy laughed, 'From now on, though, just remember, what you city slickers need is a small-town girl to show you how to do it!'

With that, Amy zipped off, running down the steps to the Subway station.

Chapter
13

Inside the Subway station, it was dark and gloomy. With all the New Yorkers safely inside their homes, the platform looked neglected and sad. From what Amy could see, the ticket-booth attendants and guards had long abandoned their posts.

Amy peered inside the empty ticket booth, and tried the door marked 'Staff'. Everything was locked up, and there was no sign of the Doctor. She made her way to the platform, but realised there were very few places left to look. However much she hated the idea, she realised there was only one way for her to go – along the tunnel itself. She stared at the psychic paper, hoping for guidance, but it was still glowing with the same message: *I'm below you.*

Was the Doctor a little bit psychic, she wondered.

Maybe it wasn't just the paper that could read minds; perhaps he could do it as well. That would explain how he was able to appear so clever all of the time – if he just read the mind of the person he was talking to and said everything they knew back at them.

Just at that moment, she thought, she could have done with something a little more helpful than *I'm below you*. Left or right? She didn't even know that much. If the Doctor was in danger, she probably had very little time, and going the wrong way might mean she got there too late. But how could she be sure?

Only one thing for it. She closed her eyes tightly, imagined the Doctor, used all she could to reach out for him with her mind…

… No. She felt nothing. Amy felt a bit stupid for even trying, and also pleased. She didn't like the idea of the Doctor being able to see inside her mind.

The decision remained. Left or right? If only something could make her choose.

The low growl made her jump. Amy opened her eyes to see an urban fox stalking out of the dark, its eyes glowing eerily blue in the shades of the station.

That made her mind up. She leapt onto the tracks and headed off to her left, away from the angry fox, walking to downtown New York the unconventional way. With all of the power in New

York out, Amy had to move slowly, feeling her way through the gloom. Oscar's torch could show her the tracks ahead, but the gaping blackness of the tunnel beyond was a forbidding mystery, and Amy had no idea what she'd find in the dark, or who might be trying to stop her getting to the Doctor.

Part of Amy wondered how she was going to save the Doctor when she got there – but she knew she had to try. She'd seen the Doctor come up with clever plans on the spur of the moment and thought to herself that she'd be as brilliant as him if she had the opportunity to do it. But nagging away at her was how helpless she'd been when Oscar was being tormented by the little midgets. Still, she'd got him out in the end. At the moment the score was Amy Pond one, Vykoids nil.

The psychic paper glowed again and Amy eagerly opened it to see the message.

If you can see this, you're going the right way. If you can't see this, then… Oh, haven't really thought that one through, have I?

Amy laughed. The message faded and then a new message came back onto it:

and HURRY UP!

This was quickly followed by:

PLEASE.

Amy started to move off, but the paper glowed yet again:

Actually, ignore me, psychic link a bit hard to control,

so I may well be wittering on a bit, but anyway, less reading, more running!

Amused at his cheek, Amy hurried along the dark tracks into the unknown. As her eyes got used to the dark, she could make out more of her surroundings. The glossy posters and adverts soon gave way to cracked plaster and crumbling bricks, curving close above her head, with strange drips of water and curious green stains. Sometimes the tunnel was close in around her; at other times it seemed cavernous and impenetrable in the gloom.

Not that Amy wanted to look too closely. Wherever the beam of her torch fell, Amy could see little furry black creatures scuttling out of the way. Rats. She told herself they were probably friendly ones. Like the one in Leadworth Primary School that they used to take home at weekends (until Ian's cat killed it). He was called Ratty, and the boys in class had liked to set him running up and down the girls' necks.

Amy hadn't been scared then, and it would take more than rats to put her off her mission now. She thought to herself how funny it was that in all the games she used to play when she was 8 years old, the Raggedy Doctor had been the one saving her from mean boys and scary rats. Now she was having to go through a dank, vermin-infested tunnel to save *him*. Amy's amusement didn't last long, as she realised she'd probably always suspected this was going to be the case. It was clear from the moment they met that he'd needed Amy Pond to sort out his life for him.

The tunnel opened out, and her torch showed a row of sidings that stretched out into the gloom. Parked up near to the line was an empty Subway train, standing idle on the tracks. For some reason seeing it sent shivers down her spine. It was like a ghost ship, or a haunted house. Something designed to be full of people felt wrong when it was quiet and so dark. It should be taking New Yorkers all the way to Coney Island, not sitting silent and still in the shadows.

The train looked far bigger and more mechanical from track level, and Amy hurried past. Unknown to her, a little pair of eyes peered out at her as she crept past. To the watching Vykoid's tiny ears, her timid footsteps sounded like the clunking boots of an unwieldy giant.

The tunnel was less flat than Amy expected. Above ground, New York may have been divided up into neat grids and numbered streets, but underneath the city the Subway sloped and twisted as it made its way from place to place.

The psychic paper glowed again.

Are you still there, Amy?

Wondering if he genuinely expected an answer, Amy looked up along the tunnel and saw a glow of light around the next bend. She raced forward, running out into a vast Subway station. Brand new and shiny, this was part of the Mayor's regeneration scheme, and it looked posher than most buildings in Leadworth. The space was dimly lit with hundreds of tiny lamps, no bigger than pencil sharpeners.

Amy approached slowly and carefully. Straining her eyes, she could see that the floor of the huge platform looked bumpy and uneven. As she moved closer, the torchlight revealed the true nature of the bumps. All along the platform, people had been tied up and covered with blankets.

Hauling herself up off the tracks, Amy crouched down beside the nearest person. His legs had been bound, and there was a gag in his mouth. Panic rose in Amy. Everywhere she looked people were lying, trussed up. The Vykoids were using this as a storage for captured humans.

A set of doors swung open, and Amy hit the ground, fast. Just in time. Out of the corner of her eye, she could see a blur of colours and high-pitched grunts of exertion as the Vykoids dropped off another load of people.

Their methods were extraordinary. A team of Vykoids would carry in a body, and lay it down for trussing by a separate group. They worked like mechanics at a Formula One pit stop. The team specialising in tying the gags around the prisoners' mouths would take a piece of cloth five times longer than they were, and spread it out like they were shaking a sheet. Then they gently lowered it over the mouth, and a separate Vykoid tied a knot behind the head. Meanwhile, a second team tied a cord around each hand and, attaching it to a miniature Vykoid crane, hauled each hand until they were floating together, zombie-like above their captive's chest.

On a signal, both hands were dropped and a waiting team of Vykoids snapped a long chain cord tightly around it. This looked like the most dangerous part of the operation, and Amy imagined that every Vykoid dreaded being responsible for cuffing the giants. The feet were taken care of by two teams of Vykoids on mini-bulldozers. They had attached special jaws to the bulldozers and, facing each other, the two bulldozers gradually pushed the ankles together. Occasionally they paused and shouted out for someone to throw more ball bearings under the ankles so they would move more easily.

Once the prisoner's feet had been pushed tight together, a mesh of nettings was dropped over the ankles, and sealed together with some sort of heat gun.

After they'd been trussed up, the bodies were shunted along to a freshly scrubbed section of platform where white-coated Vykoids opened the eyelids of the prisoners, and dropped something into their eyes, with tiny pipettes. It took two Vykoids to hold each pipette, which looked like cannons in their little hands.

Amy wasn't sure, but she thought she saw them take a lunch break during all this. And had she seen a visit from what looked like an inspector with a clipboard, or was she just cracking up under the pressure? Maybe he was a Union Rep, checking up on the minutes they'd been working, and that Health and Safety regulations were being followed.

'Wow!' Amy thought. 'They've been waiting thousands of years, and they've been planning all that time.'

She watched in awe, as twenty-five people were processed in this way in under a minute, then neatly tucked under blankets. It was as if they wanted to keep the prisoners as safe and warm as possible. Amy remembered what the Doctor had said the captured people would be used for, and shuddered in horror. Everyone around her was about to be taken to a faraway planet. They would never again see their families or eat a doughnut or drink an expensive takeaway coffee.

As soon as the Vykoids left, Amy started to untie the man next to her. He was a big bloke, still wearing his dirty work clothes and a high-visibility jacket. He was clearly a builder, dragged away from some night-time work site. Tearing off his gag, Amy saw that he was fast asleep, breathing calmly, and actually snoring a little. The drops she'd seen the Vykoids put in their eyes were probably keeping them out of it, Amy thought. And if the Vykoids were finding it that easy to process a big man like him, what chance did the rest of New York have? By the time the sun rose, New Yorkers would have been stolen from their beds and trussed up like Thanksgiving turkeys.

Another of the bodies seemed to move. Treading carefully, but still making a few people squirm as she stepped on them, Amy made her way towards it. With delight, she saw that it was the Doctor.

'Oh, here you are,' she told him. 'You could have been kidnapped to a luxury bar, or maybe the sixth floor of Macy's. But no. You chose a disgusting sewer. Again. Shall we take a minute to reflect? They caught you. Here I come, Amy Pond, saving the day!' She took the gag off the Doctor's mouth. 'Second thoughts, I could get used to this.' She put it back on. 'Only joking! I wouldn't leave you like this. Or would I?'

Amy loved the way his face went slightly flushed when he was on the back foot. She pulled the gag from his mouth again, and the Doctor looked so pleased she thought he was about to kiss her.

'Amy Pond! Never have I been so glad to see you!'

Amy leant in closer. 'What is that you have stamped on your face?'

The Doctor winced. 'Funnily enough I can't tell... Can you untie my leg?'

Amy was too busy looking at the writing on his

forehead. 'Now that is good, that is priceless. I *told* you you were skinny. Even the pint-sized invaders agree!'

Written on the Doctor's forehead, in tiny red letters, was: '*Suitable for light manual labour only.*'

Reaching through the gloop, Amy untied the Doctor's feet and retrieved the sonic screwdriver from a box, where it had been labelled '*Possible rock-cutting tool.*'

As soon as he was free, the Doctor started on Amy: 'You took your time! I was the first one they brought down here, now look at everyone here.'

Amy raised an eyebrow, not willing to be knocked off course by the Doctor. 'Ahem, avoiding the obvious here... I. Rescued. You. I think you better get used to it, Doctor, because you're going to see a whole lot more saving from me now I've got my alien-fighting moves.'

Shaking his legs back awake, the Doctor did a funny little dance to the side of the platform and pointed down. 'How come the Subway's turned off?' he asked.

'Yeah, I was getting to that. They've turned all of New York off. Those troll-faced ant-men have killed the power to the whole city.'

'Why would they do that?' the Doctor wondered. 'They're tiny, they can move fifty times faster than everything else on Earth – and they're collecting humans in Subway stations. Why, why, why? They're like an army of angry little hummingbirds, an army of vengeful, speedy, collector hummingbirds, an army of cruel, kidnapping, and murderous hummingbirds... No, your description was better.'

'I think a thank you is in order, don't you? It's all I want. I know you want to say it as well. I'll be gracious. Just try me. OK, maybe I'll be more crowing and happy. But I'll certainly enjoy how it feels. So go on!'

But the Doctor was looking around the platform, like his mind was reaching out for something that it could understand but not quite explain.

'Look at the lift,' he whispered.

The indicator above the doors showed the lift was heading down towards them. The Doctor signalled back down at the dark track. 'Come on, we better go this way. They'll be down with another batch soon.'

'Will they be OK?' Amy asked, looking at the sleeping New Yorkers, dreaming away, unaware of their fate.

The Doctor raised his sonic screwdriver, and the lift sparked and spluttered. 'We'll be back. I won't leave them. But we've got far more to find out, before we can stop the Vykoids.'

They leapt down to the track and headed back in the direction Amy had come from. Back into the gloom and dark, but away from the prying eyes of the Vykoids.

As they ran down the tracks, Amy started

laughing again. 'Suitable for light labour only – that is so funny. Even the Vykoids think you're a wimp.'

The Doctor looked hurt. 'You don't have to go to the gym three times a day and be all muscle and cropped hair to be a force to be reckoned with,' he protested.

Amy couldn't help but laugh. 'Little hint: my kind of action hero doesn't straighten his bow tie when he's trying to explain how good he is in a fight.'

They walked on in silence for a minute, both looking around them all the time for signs they were being watched, until Amy decided the Doctor had suffered enough.

'How did this work, then?' Amy waved the psychic paper at him. 'And couldn't you have been a bit clearer?'

'It's clever stuff, psychic paper. I set up an active conscious connection, very dangerous for some people, shows them what they're thinking. Plus side, it's a brilliant way to get a message to someone. If the Atraxi can send a message from their prison to Leadworth, then I can send one through a few metres of soil. Well, mainly concrete, this *is* New York. You were never that far away, just twenty metres up.' The Doctor was smiling and pointing upwards.

'What happened to you?' Amy asked.

'They dragged me here. Lucky I have these boots on. They actually stapled my trousers together. I had some kind of sedative drops put into my eye. Handily, I managed to rinse most of it out, before I got knocked out properly. I just had a quick doze...'

Amy was intrigued. 'Rinse it out? You mean you cried? The Doctor with his TARDIS and 900 years of facing beasties, actually had a good old cry when the ant soldiers got you!'

The Doctor was flustered. 'I didn't cry because I was scared... It was the only way to get rid of the tranquilliser.'

But Amy was enjoying this, and wasn't about to give up. 'Go on, tell me! What did you think about to make you sad? Was it me all alone out there, I bet it was!'

'I was being dragged by my hair through the New York Subway,' he told her. 'I didn't need to *think* of anything. Also, how come no one helped me?'

'New York on a Saturday night,' Amy said sagely. 'I suppose they'd already seen a man dressed like a geography teacher riding a mammoth through the streets.'

'What is it with you and the bow tie, Amy? Bow ties are cool!'

Amy shook her head. 'It is definitely a cry for help.'

Something was glowing in her pocket. She reached in and took out the psychic paper. 'What's this?'

The Doctor kept on walking. 'Ah, sorry, I've still got the link in place. I'll break it off now.'

But Amy had already opened the paper, and saw a message in bold letters:

SOMETHING IS COMING.

Chapter
14

'Doctor!' Amy screamed.

Through the dark of the Subway tunnel, she could hear a runaway train hurtling straight towards them.

She looked desperately around her, but they were in one of the narrower parts of the tunnel, and they had nowhere to go.

'Run!' the Doctor yelled.

Amy turned to flee, but felt the Doctor's hand on her shoulder.

'Not that way,' he shouted. 'The Vykoids are there.'

'What?' Amy screamed. 'You want me to run towards the train?'

The Doctor looked back towards the oncoming

train, now on the final stretch, and then straight into Amy's eyes. 'Trust me!'

Amy nodded. If she knew one thing, it was that she was always going to follow this man, wherever he wanted her to go.

The front of the train suddenly looked enormous. It was gathering pace as if the track tilted downhill. Amy was sure she could hear high-pitched cackles of laughter.

Just as it seemed the train would hit them, Amy felt the Doctor grab her and *throw* her into a shallow cubbyhole. She pressed up tight to the wall, as the Doctor shouted, 'Breathe in!'

With a giant clanging of machinery and metal, the runaway train came ever nearer.

The back of Amy's head was pushed against the wall. She could feel the rush of dirty hot air, and the smell of grease on steel as the front of the train skimmed past them. The skin on Amy's nose tingled as the glass and metal rushed past her, bare millimetres from her face.

Amy was sure she could make out tiny Vykoid figures racing along behind the train, looking disappointed not to have made Pond-and-Doctor Jam out of them.

'This is why you should never walk on train lines...' the Doctor said. He smiled at Amy and shone his sonic screwdriver above them. 'Still. At least it woke me up properly. Now, I'll give you a leg up – you need to grab that ladder up there.'

'Hey. Thank you, Doctor. My kind of action hero.'

The Doctor gave Amy a quick hug. 'You're the best, Pond. Now hurry up.'

With an almighty shove, Amy dislodged the manhole cover and flipped it out onto the street. Her head popped up like a ferret out of hole, and she surveyed the streets of New York.

'Ah, New York!' the Doctor exclaimed, hauling himself out after Amy. 'This is how it should be. All shops and doughnuts and pretzels, not rats and subways. I spent far too long underground last time I was here.'

They were outside Macy's on Fifth Avenue. But something was wrong. The shop windows had been smashed by looters, and the streets were deserted. There was no sign of the impromptu parties Amy had seen. Driven inside by fear, the blocks now resembled cold-war Eastern Europe. Imposing buildings, but a frightened city, scared of something they couldn't see and would never understand.

Amy was upset at how much the streets had changed. 'They were all having parties in the streets. Why are they so easy to scare off? If they just stood firm they'd be OK, those Vykoids are only wee…'

The Doctor nodded grimly. 'Fear of the invisible enemy, Amy. It can reduce anyone to weakness.'

'But what can we do?' Amy protested. 'It's not

meant to be like this! New York is all cocktails and glamour, not glass on the streets and people too scared to leave their flats.'

'Nah, it's like this most of the time. They love it, though. Tough bunch, New Yorkers. They like a city to feel edgy... Dropped by in 1829, and you should have seen the place – the Plug Ugly gang were tearing into the Dead Rabbit gang – all over Five Points. My fault, I didn't notice what was going on. We all sat down over a pack of Jammy Dodgers, and sorted it out. Well, it was either that or I sent them all back to Sligo. They soon saw sense.'

'I bet.'

'And *I* bet you're wondering what my plan is? Don't look at me like that. Of course I have one – head full of plans, me. And what I'm about to tell you is that of all the courses of action to take for fighting super-fast aliens, the most important thing is to—'

'Stop them moving so fast,' Amy cut in. 'Exactly what I was going to say.'

When they first encountered the Vykoids, Amy recalled, they'd been moving at normal speed, like tiny versions of people. It was only after the ripple of light had passed over them that the aliens had begun to move so fast. Surely it was impossible for anything to move at that speed. It was certainly going to be hard for anyone to stop the Vykoids from doing whatever they wanted.

'But we need to do more than that,' Amy pointed out. 'New York is in serious danger. No electricity, no cars, no phones, no internet. We're cut off from the outside world, and we've only got a few hours before all of New York is taken to work as slaves.'

The Doctor smiled. 'Let's go to work, then.'

Amy grinned at her action man.

The Doctor turned back and smiled like a schoolboy. 'Always wanted to say that. Something about being in America makes it cooler, don't you think?'

Amy just about stopped herself from laughing outright. 'You wish!'

Chapter
15

The main offices of the NYPD were lit with emergency storm lanterns, hurriedly dug out of storage. Even though it was the middle of the night, the place had never been so busy. Every single police officer in New York had been called in and, when all the communications had gone down, Commander Strebbins had insisted that they stay there so they were at her immediate command.

Inside her dark office, twelve breathless cadets stood in front of Strebbins. She had set up binoculars by the window to scan the dark city outside, and there was an enormous map of the streets of Manhattan spread on the table in front of her. As they spoke, she added pins into the map, building up a picture of what was happening in the city.

Strebbins gave each cadet exactly thirty seconds to report, then moved on to the next, regardless of how far they'd got in their explanations. The digital cameras she'd given them hadn't worked. It seemed that every single electrical item in New York had been disabled. With no pictures, Strebbins was snapping pencils in half, adding piles of destruction to indicate where the roads had been blocked.

'Let me get this straight,' she summarised. 'So far the roads out of action are Brooklyn Bridge, Manhattan Bridge, Williamsburg Bridge, Midtown Tunnel, Queensborough Bridge, Triborough Bridge, Third Avenue Bridge, 145th Street Bridge, you didn't go any further north, but it's safe to assume the rest are closed as well. And on the East we have Holland Tunnel, Lincoln Tunnel, George Washington Bridge, Henry Hudson Bridge. All closed by a massive blockade of debris. You say it was piles of street lamps, park benches, smashed up cars and advertising boards?'

A cadet nodded. 'They go across both lanes of every bridge I saw.'

Strebbins wasn't interested in the details and continued speaking to the room. 'Every single way in and out of the city is closed off?'

The cadets nodded in assent.

Strebbins was being very careful not to appear angry at their incompetence. 'And not one of you has any idea who did this?'

This time the nervous cadets took longer to answer. Impatient at their delay, Strebbins dismissed them without further question.

'My real men are out on the streets, they'll get this sorted. Might as well go home, the lot of you.'

One woman didn't leave with the rest of the cadets. Strebbins recognised the young woman as Yaara Stein, one of the more promising cadets.

'What is it?' Strebbins asked.

Yaara shuffled her feet nervously. 'Ma'am. I saw no troops on the streets.'

'What?' Strebbins was incredulous.

'I'm sorry, Commander,' Yaara went on quickly. 'But I saw six abandoned armoured vehicles at the exit to Brooklyn Bridge. I searched inside, but there were no signs of casualties.'

Strebbins eyed Yaara carefully. She'd read some of her carefully composed reports and knew she wasn't one to exaggerate or spread stories without reason. 'Are you telling me that my men are going missing?' Strebbins asked.

'From what I saw, ma'am, yes.'

Strebbins turned her back on Yaara and walked to the black windows, staring onto the streets below. They were twenty-three storeys up, and she had a perfect view of the streets below.

Yaara appeared at her shoulder, and handed her a pair of binoculars. 'Ten units were deployed to City Hall, ma'am. But, if you look…'

All the way along Broadway the roads were silent. Park Row was empty of patrolling troops.

'They're committed to reporting back every thirty minutes. I'll hear soon. You can go now, Yaara.'

Commander Strebbins was deeply concerned. Either every officer she had sent out was inside, pursuing the unknown aggressor, or they'd been taken somewhere. She'd thought she could cope without the gear of modern policing, the mobile phones, radios and CCTV images. But now the city was being stalked by an unseen menace, and she was losing her officers.

Yaara was hovering by the door.

'What is it?' Strebbins asked.

'Ma'am, I want you to know that I'm happy to go back on the streets. If that's what you want, that is. And I won't tell the others.'

Strebbins looked at Yaara with increased respect. She was glad she was working with such brave and dedicated people. She came to a decision. Something was keeping New Yorkers off the streets. But it wasn't her Martial Law or her curfew. It was fear. And Commander Strebbins wasn't going to let this go by unmarked.

'Yaara, call the rest of the cadets back in. We're going out together. I want to see this for myself. I'm going to pull together an armed unit so big and so strong there isn't anyone big enough to take us on.'

*

Back in midtown New York, the Doctor and Amy were standing in the Grand Hall of the Natural History Museum.

'Why are we here?' Amy asked. 'We need to get the city back to normal.'

As soon as she had told him everything she'd discovered from the police about the unveiling of the mammoth, the Doctor had insisted they return to the Museum.

'I need to know, Amy, I can't not know. We need to find out where the mammoth really came from.'

The Doctor seemed to know his way around the Museum, and Amy followed as they took turn after turn, bowling through doors marked 'Private' and 'Staff Only'.

'I used to come here quite a bit when it first opened,' the Doctor said. 'Some of the stuff they dug up in the Gobi desert! Far too unstable to put on display. My fault. I never clean up after myself.'

Amy rolled her eyes. 'You are impossible!' she complained. 'Is there anywhere you haven't been before?'

They reached a door with a plaque labelled 'S. Horwitz', and the Doctor kicked it open, with a cheery 'Howdy!'

Inside was a small laboratory. A man and a woman looked up in surprise.

'So which of you is S. Horwitz, mammoth-maker to the masses, at least according to Amy's friends in the NYPD?' the Doctor asked.

The man put his hand up, like a guilty schoolboy. 'I'm Sam Horwitz. And this is—'

'Polly Vernon,' the woman interrupted.

'You could at least look a bit pleased to see me!' the Doctor said, grinning at them.

'Please don't arrest me,' stammered Sam. 'It wasn't my fault.'

The Doctor shushed him and said reassuringly, 'I wouldn't do a thing like that, but no more hiding down here, Sam. I need you.'

Sam shook his head, evidently confused. 'I saw you riding the mammoth. I thought they'd locked you up… and you were knocked out.'

'We saw you too, Matador Man,' Amy said. 'And you were there with schoolchildren, weren't you?' she said to Polly.

'My class – I teach at an elementary school.'

'Quite a place you've got here.' The Doctor looked around the room as he talked, picking up bits of Sam's work and scanning papers. 'I do love a test tube. Amy, don't press that switch.'

Amy stopped fiddling with a wall panel, amazed as ever that the Doctor could tell anything that she was doing, even when he had his back to her.

The Doctor grabbed a chair, leapt onto it and put his feet up on the table. 'So, let's talk mammoth…'

Amy cut in to ask, 'What did the scan show?'

'You don't know, do you?' the Doctor said to Sam.

'That's odd, that's very curious.' His eyes flickered over every detail of the paper he was looking at. 'Because this is a real lab, and you're a real scientist, been to all the great academic institutions, I see – Harvard, Yale, Aberystwyth…'

While he was talking, Polly got her mobile out, trying to make a call.

The Doctor raised a finger to stop her. 'Ah, ah, ah, never mind that, not that it works anyway. But I'm the Doctor, I'm here to stop what was hidden inside that mammoth. So I need to know. If you're a real scientist, Sam, then why couldn't you tell that it wasn't a real mammoth?' As an aside he said to Amy, 'And he seems to be human, no aliens inside his belly. Or hers for that matter.'

Sam was spluttering with indignation. 'I don't know who you are, or what kind of doctor you are, and I don't know what you're suggesting. I am not part of any kind of hoax.'

The Doctor turned on his heels and made for the door. 'Thank you! That's all I needed to know.'

Sam stood up, confused. 'What do you mean?'

At the door, the Doctor turned to him. 'I scanned you, you're definitely human, all the right things in all the right places. Fear of being a failure, belief in the true nature of the mammoth, and a totally enormous crush on young Polly here.'

Amy grinned. 'You totally have to get together, you look so sweet!'

Sam blushed and shuffled slightly nervously.

Amy looked at the Doctor impishly. 'Can I?'

The Doctor nodded, and Amy ran up to Sam and knocked gently on his belly. 'No secret hatches here! And nice work on the abs may I say, you've got a keeper here, Polly.'

Amy winked at Polly, who exclaimed: 'You are both quite mad.'

The Doctor swept back into the room. 'Thank you Amy, we'll be off now, have a nice evening. I'd stay in, if I were you. But Sam, stop me if I'm barking up the wrong tree here, but I couldn't help noticing that secret map of the Dinosaur Oasis... You didn't find anything else there, did you?'

Sam shook his head.

'And it wasn't buried that far down, really, was it?'

Again, Sam shook his head. 'I knew it looked wrong, but every other detail was perfect. I thought maybe we'd made a mistake in dating the age of the ice sheet.'

'Someone put the mammoth there to be found, Sam, and now I know it wasn't you. We need your help. Next stage of the investigation into the incident is going to be pretty tricky.'

Sam seemed to brighten at this. 'What, like me using my skills as a palaeontologist to analyse the beast and work out what's happened – like they do in *CSI*?'

'*CSI: Prehistory*,' said Amy drily. 'The spin-off that's just been waiting to happen since 65 million BC.'

'There's something else at work here,' the Doctor continued, 'and you are going to be absolutely integral to our success.'

Sam nodded, biting his lower lip nervously. 'Of course, anything I can do to help. Polly, you better go straight home, this could get dangerous.'

The Doctor looked disappointed. 'What? It's Polly that we really need. Right now, Polly is the most important part of the whole plan.'

Polly was stunned. 'Why me?'

The Doctor moved in close to her. 'You've got the one thing that's going to help us stop whatever's doing this. Children!'

The Doctor led them to the roof of the Museum. Sam and Polly both gasped as they saw that New York had been plunged into absolute darkness. The streets below them were deserted.

'I've never seen the city so quiet,' Polly said.

The Doctor pointed to the skies. 'I bet you've never seen anything like that, either.'

Without the light from the buildings, the New York sky was filled with hundreds of twinkling lights. The skyscrapers seemed small in comparison to the vast size of the universe above them.

Polly shook her head in disbelief. 'I've grown so

used to seeing the night sky as an orange glow, I'd forgotten how beautiful the stars are.'

'There's the Saucepan,' Amy pointed out helpfully.

'I think it's called the Plough,' the Doctor corrected her.

'Looks more like a saucepan to me,' insisted Amy. 'Or an axe. Do aliens live there as well?'

'They're almost entirely made of water, and *so* obsessed with the weather. Very dull species. But that's not the point! There are so many worlds and solar systems, out there, Polly and Sam, things you wouldn't believe. And something very bad and very frightening has come out of that mammoth.'

Polly stared at him. 'You're both mad. Whatever has done this, the army or someone will stop them. I'm cold, it's late, and I'm going inside.'

'Not this time, Polly,' the Doctor told her gently. 'This time, it's going to be us. The army didn't last five minutes against them. Look down below, do you see anyone on the streets? Anyone at all?'

Down on the streets below, not a single soul was moving.

'They've closed down the city,' Sam said. 'It's best to wait indoors.'

'Just look at New York,' the Doctor said. 'Look. It's been driven to despair by a force that no one can see and, instead of fighting it, we're hiding. Last time I was in New York, I met men who'd been beaten down and abandoned and ruined, but they were some of the best and the bravest I've met. They had nothing left, but they were prepared to give it all. They were brilliant. Anyone who thinks they can win just because they're bigger and richer is doomed to fail. We only have one thing left. But it's a thing that will drive us on through the darkest of days to defeat the deadliest enemies the galaxy can throw at us. We are right.'

Polly and Sam were both listening attentively.

'People are disappearing from the streets,' the Doctor went on. 'You can see it with your own eyes. You don't have to trust me, but trust yourselves. You know the police should be on the streets, but they've gone too. And that means it's something very scary indeed. And what's worse, it's so hidden, we won't even know what they're planning until it happens.'

'And if we help you?' Polly asked. 'What do you want?'

'The mammoth coming back to life wasn't a miracle. This is an alien invasion, a very clever alien invasion. They're rounding up the biggest and toughest New Yorkers that they can find. So I need a team of people that can become invisible to them. I need your class, Miss Vernon. Everyone gets a chance to be a hero!'

Chapter
16

Joe Hudson rubbed his eyes to check he wasn't dreaming. Four people were standing on the fire escape outside his bedroom, high up a New York Brownstone. His teacher, Miss Vernon, the Mammoth-Man from the Museum, a girl with bright red hair, and a man with a cheeky sparkle in his eyes and floppy hair and a funny old jacket.

The man with the hair told him to open the window, and Joe slid the pane up cautiously.

'Joe, I'm the Doctor. How do you fancy saving New York?'

Joe looked at the group appraisingly. 'Are you like Iron Man?' He was 10 years old, and knew a fair bit about superheroes.

'I'm exactly like Iron Man,' the floppy-haired

man called the Doctor agreed. 'Only without the Iron. And I have two hearts. So, actually nothing at all like him, now you mention it, but that's not a problem, I'm better than him.'

'You don't even have a cape,' said Joe scornfully. He looked at the red-haired girl. 'What's your special power?'

The Doctor smiled at him. 'That's Amy. And you really don't want to know.'

Joe looked the Doctor up and down, eyeing him up for telltale signs of a hidden superpower. 'So what have you ever done, then? You're not like the Fantastic Four, are you?'

The Doctor smiled. 'Do you remember when all the clocks went to zero?'

Joe looked interested. 'They said it was a computer fault.'

'No such thing. I was there, Joe. There were aliens on Earth, and they were seconds away from destroying the planet.'

Joe was wide-eyed with astonishment.

'I didn't do it alone,' the Doctor told him. 'I needed the best people on the planet. That time it was Amy. This time it's you.'

Part of Joe wasn't surprised. With all the things that had happened over the last few years, he'd grown to believe there was something else out there. His dad still talked of the time he froze and started chanting, and nobody felt safe at Christmas now.

The Doctor put his face very near to Joe's and told him. 'There is far more out there than you could ever imagine. And everything that's happened in New York today is because of aliens. Will you help me?'

'Hell, yes!' said Joe, earning himself a disapproving look from Miss Vernon.

'That's my boy!' the Doctor grinned. Then, catching sight of Amy's expression, he decided: 'I'm not saying that again. Right, Joe, I've travelled through time and space, but right now, the only thing that's going to stop this city falling apart is you. I need someone so brave and so clever they can get around the city without anyone noticing. Do you think you can do that?'

Joe nodded, impressed that the Doctor was treating him like a grown-up. 'What about my parents?'

'They'll be better off indoors. So come on, coat, boots, whatever else you think you need to wear. Then I need you to round up everyone in your class. You're going to be my eyes and ears, Joe.'

As he clambered onto the fire escape, Joe looked at the Doctor with the awe of a private addressing a general. 'Why do you want me? Couldn't any of the others do it?'

The Doctor grinned. 'I asked Miss Vernon who was the best-behaved boy in her class, and that *so* wasn't you. I need someone *naughty*, a natural leader.'

Joe wasn't sure whether this was a good thing or not but, ready for adventures, he set off with the Doctor and his friends.

As they walked away from the building, the boy talking excitedly to the Doctor and Sam, Polly quietly asked Amy, 'So are you two dating?'

Amy scoffed at the question. 'Me and the Doctor? No way!'

Polly smiled. 'It's just you looked so together.'

Amy was shocked. She had no idea they looked like that.

Polly went on, 'You know, always laughing at his jokes, and the way you look at him like you think he's going to save the world every time he opens his mouth.'

Amy denied everything. 'Nah, he just needs me to keep an eye on him, make sure he doesn't get stolen by any tiny aliens again. I'm more of a Brad Pitt kind of girl. I'm not really one for all that floppy hair.'

Polly smiled at Amy. 'Nice try!'

They walked on in silence, until a thought struck Amy. 'Doctor, you know the story of the Trojan horse. What happened at the end? I can only ever remember the start of it.'

'They murdered everyone in Troy, and let the barbarians in through the gate,' the Doctor told her softly.

'Oh,' said Amy. 'I was always told we could *learn* from history. Fat lot of good that was. I may as well have slacked off on Friday afternoons.'

The Doctor grinned at Amy, 'Are you telling me you didn't?'

After walking in his bare feet and boxers for what felt like hours, Oscar made it back to base. With the lift out of action, he climbed all twenty-three storeys and swung open the door to an empty office. Everything was dark and quiet. His first thought was that the Vykoids had taken everyone, but it all seemed too neat. There were no signs of any kind of struggle at all. Oscar walked back into Strebbins's office and saw a handwritten note left on her desk:

'To whom it may concern. All units are on patrol. Investigating reports of missing officers.'

Oscar hit the desk in frustration. This was exactly what Amy had told him to stop. If the Vykoids took Strebbins and everyone she'd taken with her, they'd soon have every officer in New York tied up in the Subway. Not only that, but every armoured car and armed response unit in Manhattan would be out of action. New York would be cut off from the world and without defence.

On the other side of the city, the Doctor was standing in Polly's tiny apartment on Bleecker Street in Soho, talking to a group of thirty 10-year-olds. All of them had seen the mayhem caused by the Vykoids, and had emerged from their apartments eager to help the mysterious man and his friends.

Joe had told his class that the man was called the Doctor, and he was probably a bit like Bruce Wayne. Two of the boys had come out dressed as Batman, keen to take their places as protectors of the city.

'Let me tell you a story. Long ago, in the frozen Arctic wastes, an alien army landed. Only now, thousands of years later, it isn't a story. And the army is ready to attack.' The Doctor looked round at them all seriously. 'And you are the last line of defence for New York. You all saw the mammoth come to life, and everything that has happened today is because of the mammoth. The aliens are called Vykoids, they are seven centimetres tall, and they move so fast they are almost impossible to see. There is a high-intensity chronactic-delay vortex affecting the city.'

Amy nudged him in the ribs and he turned to her. 'What?'

'In English, Time Lord.'

'Ah, yes, sorry there is a Time Freeze in place over New York. Somewhere in the city, the Vykoids are broadcasting a signal that is slowing everything else down. While we're moving so slowly, they can do what they like to us. Amy saw them steal a policeman's trousers and draw glasses on his face.'

Polly's class laughed, and the Doctor added: 'I

guess it was quite funny of them, but never mind that. If we can find the source of their signal and turn it off, then they will be powerless to take us. They want to take every single adult on Manhattan and make them their slaves. Out on the streets you will see some things that will scare you, but don't be afraid. They are only here to take the biggest and the strongest. As long as you do as I say, you will be safe.'

The Doctor divided them up into pairs. 'You and you, and you and you go together. You need to stay in the shadows and keep your eyes open for anything out of the ordinary. All power is down, so any light, and sign that something is strange, you come straight back here. We need to be quick. Take the city block by block...Now over to Polly....'

Polly stared at him, caught out. She whispered to the Doctor, 'What do you mean?'

The Doctor explained 'Ah, should have told you, I need them to spread out and check every tall building in New York, go right to the top, and if they see anything that shouldn't be there, they need to run straight back here, to tell us about it. We won't be able to move far, the Vykoids will be on to us...'

'But there are hundreds of tall buildings in this city. That's impossible.'

Amy interrupted. 'They need to start at the tallest first.'

'But it'll take ages,' Sam agreed.

The Doctor joined in. 'Then I'm glad I've got the best team in New York. OK, who's for the Empire State Building? Off you go. Who's taking the Bank of America Tower? Right you two. And Batmen, I need you both on top of the Flat Iron. Take one of these each – you know what you need to do!'

They all yelled back 'Yes!' and scuttled off pair by pair, creeping like well-practised superheroes.

'What did you give them?' Amy asked.

'Fireworks! They're going to need to let us know where they are.'

'And where did you get fireworks from?'

'This is New York, Amy, you can get anything here. New Year for someone all the time, remember?'

Polly was looking worried. 'Are you sure they'll be safe?'

The Doctor answered straight away. 'The Vykoids have no interest in them. Just make sure you stay out of sight yourself. Whatever happens, don't leave your flat.' He leapt up. 'Right, off to the Zoo!'

'Come on,' Amy told Sam. 'It's your turn to be helpful.'

'Don't worry,' the Doctor said to Polly. 'We'll be barely a few minutes. Well I say minutes. We'll actually be a couple of hours, maybe even longer. But whichever way, I'll come back for you, don't forget that.'

Outside, the Doctor asked Amy to pick a car. 'I'll put it back. I didn't do anything to the other one.'

Sam was appalled. 'You can't just take someone's car!'

'Tomorrow I'll be the saviour of the city. That guy can lend me his Dodge for a few minutes.'

Amy had another question on her mind. 'How come it's not safe for Polly to be on the streets, but it's fine for me?'

The Doctor smiled. 'You're with me. Now come on, Sam. It's time we took a proper look at that mammoth of yours…'

Sam Horwitz had never broken into anywhere before, so he felt particularly naughty getting out of a stolen car and then clambering over the hastily repaired service gates of the Zoo. He'd spent most of his time studying long-dead animals, so the sounds of the Zoo at night were strange and frightening to him. Unlike the rest of New York, the animals were loving how dark the sky was, and how quiet the Zoo had become.

Passing through the happily squawking enclosures, Sam went straight to the mammoth's cage. Once inside the enclosure, Sam felt incredibly sad. The mammoth he had spent months slowly defrosting and caring for was split into two pieces. While the top half still looked like an animal you'd find in a school textbook, the lower half was a cyberpunk fantasy of metal and technology. Sam squatted down and gazed with the precision of a scientist at the inner workings of the man-made beast. He was puzzled by how they'd managed to make it look and feel so real, and pulled at the join between the metal.

Urrgggh! He stopped. The muscle was real. Some kind of lab-grown synthetic meat, perhaps. It had oozed as he'd pulled it back. Seen from the inside, the fur was obviously fake. Everything about the hairs seemed real, but just under the skin, was hard, flexible armour. The Vykoids had made the mammoth far tougher than any other creature it might meet.

The Doctor finished examining the tusks, and moved on to the eyes.

'They did beautiful work here. A real cornea, plus technology. It's not surprising you didn't spot it was a fake. Now, Sam, as much as I love your approach, it's time to get brutal. We need to make a bit of room in this thing. Can you smash all of that out?' He was pointing to the gracefully constructed central section of the mammoth.

Sam started carefully dismantling the Vykoid living quarters that took up most of the beast.

'Er, Sam, tick-tock, tick-tock, time is the one thing we don't have a lot of.'

Amy stepped in to help. 'I think what he means is do it more like this…'

Kicking with her boots, Amy smashed a delicate level of the Vykoid ship, sending the hand-crafted construction skittering to the floor in tiny pieces.

Taking care to leave the controls in the head of the mammoth untouched, Sam set about his work with a vengeance. This was the mammoth that had ruined his career, and he'd suddenly realised he was going to enjoy taking it to pieces.

'Does he do this a lot?' he asked Amy.

'Well, I've never seen him with a mammoth before,' Amy answered.

Sam loved that Amy had such spirit. Before he'd met the Doctor, Sam had been ready to hide from the world for ever, content never to show his face in public again. But now he was gleefully breaking into the City Zoo and dismantling an alien spaceship. 'I meant, does he just not tell you what he's planning to do,' he clarified.

'I know,' said Amy with a quiet smile.

'I guess he's doing this so the Vykoids can't leave,' Sam suggested.

'Maybe. But it's more likely he doesn't know what he's doing yet. Just has a kind of feeling for something…'

Sam wasn't entirely reassured by this.

His doubts grew even stronger when the Doctor stood back from the mammoth, and asked, 'Enough room for a man inside there yet?'

Sam told him there was, and the Doctor nodded. 'Go on then.'

'Excuse me?'

'In you get, Sam Horwitz.'

Amy watched Sam carefully. She could see him struggling with his instincts. There was something so compelling about the Doctor, she was fascinated to see the effect he had on people.

'You want to shut me in there, don't you?' Sam guessed.

'No, that would be silly. I just want to see what happens when you get inside.' The Doctor smiled at Sam. 'Of course, now you say it, shutting you in for a bit could help us learn a lot.'

Amy nudged Sam towards the door. 'Come on, in you go, no time like the present.'

'You'll be out soon,' the Doctor assured him. 'In fact, the sooner you're in, the sooner you'll be out again.'

Unable to resist the lunatic logic, Sam found himself doing something he'd never imagined. Putting his head up into the chest of the mammoth, he hauled his body up on the metal innards, tucking his legs up inside the space he'd smashed out.

Below him, the Doctor and Amy took one side of the mammoth's belly and lifted it high into position. Sam heard a quiet click as it shucked into position. From the outside, he guessed, the Polar Woolly Mammoth once again looked very, very real.

But inside the dark of the mammoth, Sam was growing increasingly angry. The Doctor had promised he'd be out soon, but minutes were crawling past. He was hot, he was suffocating, and he was furious that they had tricked him like this. Sam banged on the metal belly, determined to smash his way out.

But nothing would budge. He shouted for them to release him from his curious prison, but he heard no sounds outside.

For all Sam knew, they had left him there at the mercy of the Vykoids. His mind raced at a hundred miles an hour, and his anxiety spun out of control – what if the Vykoids came back and found him in their ship? What would they do when they saw what he'd done to it?

Finally after ten nervous minutes, Sam heard another click, and the belly of the mammoth was disconnected. Sam was so eager to get out, he stamped down on the metal, and fell out in a sprawling mess, landing heavily on the floor of the Zoo enclosure.

The Doctor and Amy were astonished.

'What's got into you?' Amy asked, upset that Sam was so cross at them.

'You left me in there for ages!' Sam screamed, desperate to get his frustration off his chest.

'That's interesting.' The Doctor was talking more to Amy than to Sam. 'It's made of Vykoid technology. So it's immune to the Time Freeze.'

'You were only in there for a minute,' Amy explained, 'but we're all being slowed down by the Vykoids. In there you must have been going at normal speed.'

'So this means we can fight them at their own speed!' Sam exclaimed, realising that his ordeal had not been in vain.

'Yes,' the Doctor agreed. 'But only if we all get inside the mammoth.'

'You cannot be serious?' Amy stared at the Doctor. 'You are, aren't you? I should have known!'

Chapter
17

Commander Strebbins was having a very bad night.

First, a mammoth had come alive, destroying the Grand Hall of the most famous museum in New York. Then the city had blacked out. Now she was losing units of men, all over the city. Her decision to go onto the streets herself had been popular with her officers. They had been scared by reports of an unseen enemy, and were worried for their colleagues.

But now she was at the helm they felt protected. Patrolling the streets like an American Boadicea, Strebbins had her head poking out of the top of an armoured vehicle, surveying all the damage to the streets as she went.

'Take me to City Hall,' she hollered down to her

driver. 'I want to see this for myself.'

The convoy rolled along the empty streets like an army conquering a ghost town. Strebbins had never seen the city like this, and she was determined to restore it to its roaring, all-night-long self.

On the lawns of City Hall, Lieutenant Red of the Vykoid army lowered a tiny telescope and smiled with triumph. He'd seen their main prize – the human identified as running the city, Commander Jackie Strebbins.

She was the woman who had put the city under Martial Law. If they took her, they could do what they wanted. Red signalled for his men to spread out across the road. Working at top speed, they unrolled nets across every stretch of sidewalk, and a specialised climber Vykoid ran a cord up to a pivot point on the fifth floor of City Hall. Meanwhile, a team of twenty Vykoids leapt into a human jeep and, with different teams on each pedal, manoeuvred it into position. The trap was set...

Strebbins pulled up in front of City Hall, the car jolting to a stop to avoid a water main bursting a fountain over the sidewalk. On her signal, the officers piled out of the back of the van.

Yaara seemed immediately unnerved. 'Ma'am, there's something on the road.'

Commander Strebbins was already climbing

down from her vantage point. 'I'm sure I've stepped on worse in my time,' she said drily.

But as her feet hit the ground, they stuck to it firmly. It was as if her shoes were made of Velcro. She tugged and yanked with all her might, but she couldn't move.

'Eyes all round!' Strebbins commanded, determined that she would not be ambushed like this.

Somewhere close by, an engine fired up. A jeep zoomed away from City Hall, pulling with it the cord that gathered up the huge nets that Strebbins and her officers were standing on.

The nets had been designed to subdue a Tyrannosaurus Rex, so Commander Strebbins didn't stand a chance. As either side of the nets pulled up, the entire unit of armed police officers was bundled together. Like rabbits caught in a trap, they were dragged into the air, legs and arms poking through the holes in the net. They were helpless.

Deep underground in a Subway station, General Erik inspected the work of his Vykoid scientists. He'd been forced to adapt his battle plan to the unfortunate mistiming of their arrival, and he was more than happy with what he'd come up with. His original mission had called for very few slave workers to be captured. But if his new plan worked, he'd be bringing home all of New York.

When they'd discovered that their cryogenic sleep units had malfunctioned and they'd woken up thousands of years too late, he could have abandoned the mission and gone home. He wouldn't have been blamed. Instead, he'd sent out a team of Vykoids with a mission: find a human and force it to take the mammoth to the greatest city on Earth. He'd faced a threat of mutiny from the disgruntled soldiers eager to go home and a vote of no confidence from the Vykoid Fleet Commanders, but he'd persisted with his plan, and it had worked. However powerful and well defended New Yorkers thought they were, Manhattan was defenceless to a hidden enemy.

He signalled to the Chief Scientist with a brief wave of his hand. 'Please begin.'

In a corner of the Subway station, the Vykoids had assembled something that looked like a shower in a hippie commune. They had constructed a man-sized chamber out of bent copper pipes and elaborate woodwork built into the wall.

Hauling on levers and pulleys, the Vykoids were lifting something large into a standing position in the chamber. On either side of the object, platforms of Vykoids waited to be called into service. Waiting like paratroopers before a drop, they had a hint of bullishness and anxiety, overridden by the sense that this was their moment. After years of waiting inside the mammoth, they were finally getting to put their technology into action. It wasn't how they had expected to use it but, deep down, they knew it was going to be a lot more fun.

Centuries of being frustrated by their size had led the Vykoid race to become experts in building larger vehicles. But even with the might of technology on their side, the universe still refused to take them seriously and so, with the logic of the conqueror, they had decided to use their machines to subdue anyone that stood taller than them.

Their perfect machines of war had run amok through solar systems and caused chaos across galaxies. All the time, the best brains of the Vykoid race had been working long and hard on a new and better solution to the problem of being tiny in a world of oafs and gangly gargantuans. They had learnt how to control the minds of larger animals, to take charge of their every action.

A bright spotlight blazed onto the object in the Vykoid conversion cubicle. It was Commander Strebbins, fast asleep and tied upright to a wooden scaffold by hundreds of tiny ropes.

Buzzing with adrenalin, Lars, a Vykoid private on his tour of duty, hopped into a minute seat and saluted his commander. The chair was packed with hundreds of controls. At his left hand were dozens of buttons, and on his right a carved Vykoid joystick.

The scientists around him backed away, and Lars shouted out, 'Ready!'

With a dazzling manoeuvre, Lars was shot into

the air to land squarely on the head of the NYPD commander.

General Erik watched with satisfaction as Strebbins's left eye opened halfway. Then her right eye jammed wide open in a thousand-yard stare.

Lars radioed down to the command centre. 'I'm having slight ocular control difficulties, sir.'

A Vykoid scientist spoke into a communicator. 'You're doing great, just blink it out, and relax the muscles.'

Two sleepy-eyed blinks later, and Lars was back in business. He attempted a smile, and the Commander grinned dumbly around the room. Her lips trembled, and then opened in ludicrously fast speech. 'Hey, it ain't easy being this big! Talk about dumb animal…'

Down below, the Vykoid scientists were drenched in drops of spittle.

The lead scientist, spoke into the communicator again. 'Hat back on… now.'

With a skilful whirring of pulleys, the NYPD cop baseball cap was delicately lowered into position. A dangling Vykoid tided up the hair around the cap and gave a thumbs-up signal to down below. Lars was now out of sight, and totally in command of Commander Strebbins.

'I'm good to go.'

Lars marched Strebbins out awkwardly, as the Vykoid scientist called out, 'Next!'

General Erik and his Vykoids had felt hours pass, stopping for two meal breaks and nine cups of coffee in the process. But in only thirty minutes of New York human time, the Vykoids had upgraded themselves to become controllers of hundreds of fully armed NYPD cops. They had taken the defenders of the city, and made them the attackers.

Chapter
18

Leaving the Doctor and Sam to rip more parts out of the mammoth, Amy wandered out to Fifth Avenue to watch out for fireworks from Polly Vernon's class. The sun was beginning to rise above Brooklyn, sending fingers of light through the still clear sky.

Then, as the sun rose over the park, something unexpected happened. Another huge pulse of green light spread over the city. Just like before, Amy felt as if every part of her had become weightless, like she'd reached the top of a rollercoaster ride. It passed just as quickly and, all around New York, the power returned.

On the street around her, cables ripped from street lamps sparked on the tarmac, and the windows of the city flashed into light again, the blackness banished. It was astounding to Amy how quickly the air filled with chatter as all the televisions and radios that had been left on around the city blared noisily back to life.

Hearing the commotion, the Doctor ran out of the Zoo to where Amy was staring joyfully at the rejuvenated city, hopeful that the threat was over.

'Hey, the lights have come back on!' she cried. 'Is it over? Maybe we've got the better of them?'

A department store window showed TV screens with news channels scrambling to get their reporters on air. The rolling headlines were calling it the Big Blackout. The sun was rising above Brooklyn, and the dark night was over. All the noises and business of an ordinary New York day began to fill the air, as if the long dark night had been an aberration or a bad dream. New York had survived a night of terror and confusion and it felt like a time to celebrate.

But the Doctor punctured Amy's feeling of elation. 'That was too easy,' he told her grimly. 'The Vykoids haven't done what they came to do. This all has to be part of their plan. The next stage has just begun.'

As New Yorkers ventured out of their apartments, Amy could hear mobile phones ringing as people checked on their friends and families. 'Are you OK?' 'What did you see?' 'Is anyone hurt?' All around New York the same things had happened. But no one seemed to know who had done this, or why such mayhem had been caused.

The Doctor and Amy joined a crowd watching the television news through a cracked department-store window. Trinity Wells was broadcasting to the nation, looking immaculate as she spoke into camera.

'I'm about to bring you an exclusive for AMN news. The woman who took control of the city overnight, and has brought order back to New York, joining us live, is Commander Strebbins of the New York Emergency Crisis Taskforce.'

Strebbins walked stiffly into the studio and sat beside Trinity.

'So,' said Trinity Wells, 'Commander Strebbins, what happened last night? And what should New Yorkers be doing this morning?'

Commander Strebbins leaned into the camera, looking rather awkward, her make-up smudged and uneven. When she spoke, her lips dribbled spittle, but the words came out clear. 'I am keeping the curfew on Manhattan with all bridges and tunnels into the city remaining closed. Following the damage last night, we need to do structural tests before they will be safe to re-open. However, I am pleased to tell you that the City is otherwise back to normal: Metro lines will start running at 8 a.m., and schools and places of work are expected to open as usual. I'd like to reassure all small business owners that there will not be a repeat of the violence and looting of last night, and that there is no cause for concern.'

'How come she managed it, and we didn't?' Amy asked the Doctor. She could tell that something wasn't right. 'Maybe they've turned off, like in *War of the Worlds*, or the atmosphere poisoned them, or something. They should have worn little Vykoid gas masks…'

The Doctor didn't answer, and Amy was soon distracted by the television. 'What is wrong with Trinity Wells, though? Not a great day for her fashion-wise… I think her shirt is on inside out.'

The Doctor leant in close to the television.

Amy tried again for a reaction from him. 'And why is she wearing that ridiculous hat? What does she think she looks like?'

The camera cut back to Commander Strebbins. She was telling Trinity with evident pride that her team had been working throughout the night to restore power and had successfully apprehended the insurgents responsible. There was a quick shot of some tired-looking men being hurried into a police van, ragged in boiler suits and red-eyed. Then Strebbins went on to explain again that the city was safe. That it would always be safe, and New York could rely on having the biggest and best Police Department in America.

'She's got all the wrong people,' Amy protested. 'She's mad, she'll try and shoot anything that moves.

I bet she's rounded up everyone who can't defend themselves. It's outrageous!'

The Doctor had become very pensive. 'Oh, Amy, I think I've missed something very important... I should have seen it... How did I ever think they'd actually make all those people *slaves*? Especially when they came here looking for Triceratops and Diplodocuses to haul rocks for them. I don't think that's Commander Strebbins at all. We've been doing what they wanted all along! They put the best people they had out on the streets, and now they're under Vykoid control.'

'Explain?' Amy demanded.

'Last night every single police officer in New York went onto the streets and disappeared.'

Amy realised what he meant. 'Now they're all back, walking a bit funny, and telling us to carry on as normal.'

'That's clever,' the Doctor marvelled. 'They created the threat. Made everyone hide indoors. Now the police are the heroes of the hour, and they're going to line the streets and pretend to save everyone.'

The TV screen was now showing Grand Central Station. Hundreds of police officers were standing on every side of the road.

Trinity Wells announced: 'The streets of Manhattan will be protected today by thousands of special forces...'

The Doctor turned to Amy. 'We have to stop this. All of New York is about to be dragged into slavery by its own leaders, and no one will believe a word we say.'

'But how are they going to do it? They've only got a mammoth, and they left it at the Zoo.'

'If they're advanced enough to put a Time Freeze over all Manhattan, they must be a Level 18 civilisation, maybe higher. They don't need that old mammoth any more. New York's built on grids, very regular pattern, pretty easy to map a high-intensity teleport matrix on top of this place. They'll take everyone that's out on the streets. And at 9 a.m., seven million people will be on the streets of New York. They'll be sitting ducks.'

Amy plunged in with her own ideas. 'So, we get Sam, recall the police, let everyone know what they're up to, and shut down the transmitter. Whenever our gang of kids finds it.'

The Doctor didn't answer. Amy looked round and was infuriated to see that he'd wandered off.

She ran to catch up with him, 'Oi! Where are you going? Oh…'

The Doctor was facing a line of NYPD officers, who were pointing their guns straight at him. As one, they stiffly raised their arms and took off their hats. Sitting under the baseball cap of each trooper was a tiny Vykoid, grinning and waving at the Doctor and Amy.

Amy tugged at his arm. 'Er, Doctor. Are we the only people in New York who know they're not really the police?'

'I see your point,' the Doctor agreed. 'In that case we should *run*!' They hurtled off down the street with the police-Vykoids following stiffly behind.

'Slow down, Doctor!' Amy called out. 'They can barely walk, let alone run!'

The Doctor looked back and saw the police waddling towards them with stiff legs making awkward strides. The Vykoid controllers were doing their best, but somewhere deep down, the police minds were fighting against them, slowing their movements.

'It's not them I'm worried about,' the Doctor told Amy, pointing to the other side of the road, where a fleet of armoured police vans were pulling up.

'Ah. Point taken.' Amy took the Doctor's hand, and they fled across a crossroad, dodging taxis and bikes.

Amy saw a yellow taxi idling outside an office and leapt into the back. The Doctor had a better idea and jumped into the driver's seat. At a nearby coffee stand, the driver saw them, and shouted 'Oi!' He headed towards them, waving his hands like a drunk Italian.

'Museum, please,' Amy requested, leaning back in the cab. 'Try to avoid the avenging aliens, though, if you could.'

'Yes, ma'am.' The Doctor slammed the accelerator down and they sped off, heading through early morning Manhattan.

Close on their tail, four NYPD cars were slamming through the traffic, sirens blaring and lights flashing. Amy could see the nearest driver had taken his hat off, and his Vykoid controller was whooping with excitement, full of the glory of the chase. They might have come to Earth to round up mammoths, but were equally at home hunting Time Lords in New York.

Reaching a red light, the Doctor slammed on the brakes and turned unexpectedly to the right, tyres smoking on the tarmac as they skidded round the corner. Behind them, one of the cars shot off the road, ploughing into a marble building.

'One down, Doctor…' Amy called. 'I didn't know you could drive like this!'

The Doctor swung the car to the right, heading up a narrow back alley. 'I don't often get the chance!'

The remaining squad cars were still close behind, and were gaining on them. A shot rang out, and Amy heard the terrifying sound of bullet tearing through metal. To compensate, the Doctor tried to weave their car from side to side, looking like an out-of-control learner driver.

Reaching a main road, the Doctor shot straight out, aiming for another back alley. This time he clipped a newspaper stand as he took a short cut on the pavement, sending copies of the *New York Times* flying through the air.

The Doctor's driving had taken them into the lurking industrial buildings of Hell's Kitchen, and he turned through more gloomy side streets. As the taxi approached, suspicious workers carrying unmarked crates retreated back into the shadows, unnerved by the sound of police sirens. Amy could see only one car on their tail now, and that seemed to be losing ground. The Doctor turned the taxi onto Broadway and joined the streams of cars.

'It's still with us,' Amy told the Doctor, and he spun the taxi around to the right. The car was heading straight for Central Park and, without warning, the Doctor veered onto the grass, smashing through a fence and circling the lake.

'What are you doing?' Amy yelled at the Doctor.

'I've lost them, haven't I?'

When she looked round, Amy had to agree that he was right. 'But we're in the middle of nowhere... Oh.' While she'd been talking, they'd arrived back at the entrance to the Zoo.

Parked right in front of the Zoo, Oscar was sitting in a squad car packed with schoolchildren. Amy leapt out and ran to hug him, then checked herself. *What if he's one of the Vykoids now?* Oscar's happiness at seeing Amy was tested when she yanked his hat off, ruffled his hair, and then poked him repeatedly.

'Good, it *is* you!' Amy said with relief, and gave him a huge hug. 'Although what's with the normal clothes? I thought a tiara suited you.'

'What are you doing with our team?' the Doctor asked.

'I found them downtown trying to set light to something,' Oscar explained. 'They told me you'd put them up to it. There's a lot of folk going missing right now, so I thought I'd bring them back to you…'

Oscar opened the car door and the sleepy children in the back of his car leapt out and ran to the Doctor. Joe, another boy who was dressed as Batman, and two girls surrounded the Doctor and Amy, talking over each other excitedly.

'We've found it.'

'It's this massive glowing ball.'

'Do I have to go to school now?'

'Joe didn't see it first, it was me.'

'We need to get a boat.'

'Speak slower!' Amy told them. 'One at a time.'

Joe stepped forward. 'We went up the Chrysler Building, and Millie got scared but it was only the wind. Then we went down to CitiGroup, and went out on the roof, and we could see it… It's the Statue of Liberty. Everywhere else is dark, but there's something inside the top of it, like a giant fireball that kept on burning.'

'It was green,' Millie added.

The Doctor beamed at them. 'That is brilliant, Joe. You have been the best. Truly the best.'

Joe's face lit up with joy.

'I'm going to send you back to Miss Vernon now,' the Doctor went on. 'Whatever you see, just stay indoors.'

Amy looked downtown, gazing down the lonely deserted streets strewn with rubbish. Every road was covered with detritus of the Vykoids' midnight rampage, and she knew that every obstruction might be hiding the alien army, lurking and ready to ambush them.

'Don't worry,' the Doctor said. 'We're three kilometres and a short ferry ride away from the Statue of Liberty and, if we don't get there before New York wakes up, all of Manhattan are going to be taken as slaves. I guess you're going to get to see the sights of New York after all, Amy.'

Chapter
19

Inside the Zoo, the Doctor flung open the gates of the mammoth enclosure and stood in front of the enormous beast. Amy could see what he was thinking. And she flatly refused.

'*This* is your plan? No way.'

'Come on.' The Doctor started to clamber up inside the mammoth, and beckoned for Amy to join him.

'There's an army of them! Every police officer in New York will be trying to stop us. They have guns.'

'Forget the courage of the mob. We have the single-mindedness of the foolishly hopeful!'

'I'm not coming in unless it's bigger on the inside,' Amy insisted. 'If I have to face the tiny army, I'm going to do it with dignity.'

'It's definitely faster in here,' the Doctor said. Leaning back out, he looked sweatier to Amy. 'You still here? I just spent half an hour fixing it so I can steer with this.' He held up a pretzel he'd picked up from a shut-down stall. 'Isn't that funny! Steering with a pretzel? No? Nothing? Not even a little bit?' He wasn't getting any reaction from Amy. 'Anyone ever tell you that you're hard to please?' he asked.

Amy smiled. 'All of them, Doctor.' She had made a decision. 'Now budge over. If we're going in this thing, I'm driving.'

She grabbed the Doctor's hand and hauled herself up. The Doctor had smashed out a space in the neck of the mammoth, and Amy squeezed through the gap, emerging into the empty head of the mammoth. The beast's massive eyes were windows onto the city, and she gasped in amazement.

Outside, everyone was moving in ultra-slow motion. It was like she was seeing people frame by frame. Joe was standing beside Oscar, casually picking his nose in a gesture that seemed to go on and on. Amy was drawn into the sheer graphic wonder of seeing everything in such slow motion. Behind Joe, two chatting women looked like lazy Guppy fish, mouthing aimlessly. Amy was sure she could see every muscle on Oscar's neck as he breathed. Oh so slowly, he was getting the children back into the police car to deliver them to Polly.

'Is this what's it's like for the Vykoids?' Amy asked. 'No wonder they've got so far.'

'If we can get to the Statue of Liberty and break their signal, they'll be helpless.'

'Why did you say, *if*?' Amy cut straight in, a hard note to her voice.

'What do you mean?'

'Don't pretend! You said, "*If* we can get there". We've just climbed inside an alien spaceship disguised as a mammoth, and you're not sure if it's going to work?'

'The one thing we have is the element of surprise. No one in their right mind would attempt to do what we're going to do.'

The Doctor wired the pretzel to a set of tiny Vykoid controls and pulled back. The mammoth lifted its head, and Amy could see the skyline of New York ahead of her, the Chrysler Tower glinting in the morning sun.

'Whoa!' Amy could feel herself starting to slip backwards. The Doctor had pulled too far, and the mammoth reared up on its back feet.

Looking through the huge eyes again, Amy watched Sam running incredibly slowly to witness the sight of the mammoth at full stretch.

'Down, Doctor!' Amy snapped, and pushed the pretzel-wheel forward. With that, the mammoth crouched down and lowered its head. Amy felt a judder as the enormous tusks dug into the ground.

The Doctor lowered the belly, and stuck his head out. 'Sam – where have you been? We need you. Can't quite get a grip of the steering.'

'I noticed that.' Sam pointed at the trenches the tusks had gouged in the ground.

'Good, in that case you'll understand what you need to do. No one knows a mammoth like you.'

Sam took the Doctor's hand and scrambled up, squeezing through the neck to join Amy.

But the Doctor raised his hand. 'Uh, uh, sorry Sam, turns out those Vykoids borrowed a trick from the dinosaurs. Two steering centres, one in the front, the other in the…'

'So you got me up here to go in the back end?' Sam was deflated.

The Doctor clapped him on his shoulders. 'Good man! Don't worry, you can still see out.'

'How?' Sam asked, and then suddenly realised. 'Oh…'

'What a team we'll be! So, Sam, if you see us going the wrong way, just shout.'

The Doctor crouched by the left eye and grabbed the pretzel-wheel. But Amy shoved him over. 'I'm steering, remember? You had your turn in the taxi.'

Amy felt happier at the wheel. After all, she'd meant their trip to New York to be the time when she stopped being bossed around, and here she was, about to drive a mammoth down Broadway. She gave the controls a gentle pull, and the mammoth rose to its feet. Then, with another subtle shunt from Amy, it started to walk forward, the machinery whirring as its steps landed heavily on the tarmac.

The mammoth walked slowly out of the Zoo, past the elephant enclosure and out of the main gates.

'I'm going to see if I can get this moving a bit faster,' the Doctor decided. He took out a pen and started tapping at the tiny Vykoid controls. Lights started flashing all around them.

'What have you done?' Amy asked. 'That looked pretty random to me.'

The Doctor looked hurt. 'As if I'd be so— Whoa!'

While he was speaking, the mammoth had crouched low to the ground, pushed off with its left feet, and rolled over onto its back.

'You were saying, Doctor?' Amy yelled, her head squashed up against the floor.

The mammoth kept rolling over, but when it came back to horizontal it just kept on going.

'Can't you stop it?' Amy demanded.

The Doctor was bent double, his gangly legs waving in the air.

Amy leant forward and yanked the pretzel-wheel. It came off in her hands.

From behind, Sam came tumbling in and collided with the Doctor. As the mammoth turned over and over, their arms and legs flailing around the mammoth's head. The Doctor's arm hit a minuscule lever, and the mammoth stopped.

'Finally!' Amy dusted herself down. 'I told you to let me steer…'

Sam pointed through the window. They had come to rest in the partially drained Central Park Pond.

Amy wasted no time. Winding the controls around the pretzel again, she got the mammoth to leap to its feet and stagger out of the park. Early risers walking their dogs in the park saw a soaking wet and mud-splattered mammoth appearing from the pond and fled.

Amy steered the beast to Fifth Avenue, and soon found it was easier to step over cars and rubble than to walk around. Going through the Pulitzer Fountain, she paused by Bergdorf Goodman's and swung the mammoth's head to get a closer look.

'Oops! Didn't mean to do that.' She'd smashed the department store's window with the mammoth's tusks. She hurriedly put the mammoth back on course.

Amy pressed forward down the wide Fifth Avenue, and the mammoth started to pick up speed. Past the Bank of America and Tiffany's the mammoth galloped, so fast the buildings became a blur. Clutching the pretzel-wheel, Amy stayed focused on the road ahead. From the left eye she could see security guards turning in her direction, but they moved so slowly that they didn't even see her before the beast had sprinted past.

'Remember they can't actually move out of the way,' the Doctor said. He pointed ahead at a group of people crossing the road so slowly they looked like the cover of the Beatles' *Abbey Road* album.

'Got it covered, Doctor,' Amy assured him. She leaned back in her seat, and the mammoth reared up and leapt over the people's heads, spraying them with muddy water.

Racing past Macy's, Amy had arrived at the junction with Broadway when the Doctor yelled 'Stop!'

He pointed to the left. Madison Square was filled with NYPD troops, and Strebbins was marching up and down, barking out orders.

Hundreds of Vykoid soldiers were gathering, setting up for the next stage of the operation. Their tiny jeeps were parked up on the curb, and they seemed to be synchronising their watches. For the first time since the Time Freeze had started, Amy could see the Vykoids moving at normal speed. The little aliens started to run over as soon as they saw the mammoth, and she tensed up.

'It's OK,' the Doctor reassured her. 'They're no faster than us now.'

The Vykoids were looking very alarmed, and started making calls on their tiny walkie-talkies.

'On we go!' the Doctor said, and Amy steered the mammoth away from the Vykoids and down Broadway.

A breathless Sam stuck his head up into the mammoth's neck and asked: 'Shouldn't we have hidden from them?'

Amy and the Doctor burst out laughing.

'We're in a mammoth on Broadway,' Amy pointed out. 'I don't think subtlety and camouflage are among our strengths!'

As they headed into downtown New York, Amy gazed at the vast city around her. There were NYPD officers at the corner of each block. To a girl from Leadworth, the casual display of guns was shocking. And Amy knew what they were going to use them for. Passing City Hall, she saw a crowd of people waiting on the steps.

'The Vykoids are sealing all the doors to keep everyone out in the open,' the Doctor said.

'Talk about mean streets... How long do we have?'

The Doctor looked around. 'They'll wait until they get it at the busiest time. Everyone in Manhattan will go to work and end up as a mining slave...'

High above Manhattan, General Erik gazed out of the crown of the Statue of Liberty and saw the city waking up. Pretty soon, he would instruct his men to use the police on the streets to lead everyone in New York onto Broadway.

General Erik's Vykoid soldiers had worked through the night to lay teleport signal amplifiers along its length and, when the tarmac was packed to bursting, he would send the first shipment back. If the NYPD did their work as planned, they would slowly empty the city, forcing everyone to march onto Broadway and go to his hometown.

At moments like this, General Erik wondered if he'd aimed too low. He was already confident in his success, and was seriously considering extending the campaign to round up the entire East Coast of America. He'd get promoted for this operation, he was sure.

More than anything, General Erik loved that he'd been able to do all this, with none of the humans suspecting anything was happening until the very last minute. With any luck, he would take Manhattan without a single loss of life.

A nervous private interrupted General Erik's thoughts. 'Sir, the mammoth is on the move. And Sector 9 is reporting the non-human we encountered called the Doctor was not part of the Puppet Programming Operation.'

General Erik dismissed the private, and turned back to the window. He felt unshakeable. There was nothing one man and a mammoth could do now.

With the children safe at Polly Vernon's, Oscar stepped back into his squad car. Ever since he'd seen Amy stride off into the Subway, he'd been determined to prove himself. He couldn't bear to watch his fellow officers turned into Vykoid slaves. Hardening his heart to the task ahead, he told himself that his only option was to find Commander Strebbins and take the alien controller from her head. Taking out his mobile, he dialled the private number Strebbins had given him.

On the other side of the city, walking stiffly out of the TV Studio, Commander Strebbins picked up her phone.

'I am ready to report on the Doctor,' Oscar told her.

Sitting in the command chair on top of her head, the Vykoid Lars grinned and waggled his levers to make Strebbins answer. 'Of course, I'll be at Madison Square. Meet me there.'

Sitting in his car, Oscar's hands shook with nerves. He'd never thought being a police officer would lead him to this. He drew out his gun and loaded it. He wasn't going to let New York go down without a fight.

Chapter
20

Their mad dash across Manhattan had worked, and Amy stopped the mammoth in the shadow of the World Financial Center. The waters of the Hudson lapped at the quayside in front of them. The dock was thronging with boats, and New York ferries. Amy was eager to get out of the mammoth and leap aboard.

'Hang on a minute, Amy,' said the Doctor, then yelled back to Sam: 'Is this thing waterproof?'

Sam appeared, ruffled and shiny from being cooped up in the back end of the mammoth. 'It should be, yeah. I mean, it kept the ice out for all that time.'

The Doctor knocked on the walls, 'Built of rare Vykoid alloys. I reckon it'll float, even with us inside.

Oh don't look at me like that, Amy, that's the slowest ferry you'll ever see. It'll be like the open bus tour of Leadworth. This way, we get to find out one of the lost secrets of prehistory… Can a mammoth swim?'

Amy turned the mammoth away from the ferry, and headed south into Battery Park. In front of her they could see Ellis island, where twelve million immigrants had once arrived for a new life in America and, standing proudly in the bay, the Statue of Liberty itself.

Joe and the other children had been right. Even in the morning sun, Amy could see the pulse of alien light on the Statue. Sparks of green energy arced between the spikes of the crown, and the top of the statue crackled like a circuit waiting to discharge.

'OK, I'm ready,' Amy said. 'Though I'd like to point out you never said it was going to be "Goodbye Leadworth, hello drowning inside a hairy elephant".'

The Doctor smiled. 'Being trapped inside friendly monsters is all part of the fun.'

The mammoth picked up pace, going faster and faster until it reached the water's edge. Amy pulled back on the pretzel-wheel, and the giant creature soared forward.

Barely a metre away from the quay, they landed in the water with a massive splash and, for a disconcerting moment, the entire mammoth sank down, down into the murky waters of the Hudson.

As water rose up past the eyes of the mammoth, Amy saw an astonished school of fish blinking in wonder at the hairy beast.

Amy looked around her nervously. 'Er, how exactly do you know Vykoid metal floats?'

'The skin is holding tight,' the Doctor reassured her. 'Look, no water's leaking in. So come on – teach this thing to swim!'

Amy kicked out with the mammoth's feet, and it sprang off the silty riverbed and bobbed back up to the surface, its massive tusks jutting out of the water.

As the head broke the surface of the water, a slow-moving seagull flapped its wings lazily and took to the air. The Doctor grabbed the pretzel-wheel and yanked the controls to one side.

'We're going a bit faster than them, too – they can't move out of the way,' he explained.

The seagull narrowly avoided being impaled on the fast-moving tusk and splashed back down in the water, perturbed by the hairy beast wallowing in the Hudson.

'Full steam ahead!' the Doctor yelled.

Battling through the waves and currents the mammoth was swimming directly towards Liberty Island. It lurched side to side with the swell and was beginning to gather all the rubbish from the water in its long coat.

'This is fun, isn't it?' the Doctor said to Amy.

'Maybe we could keep this in the TARDIS when we're done?'

Amy was too busy keeping the mammoth afloat to pay him much attention. 'I so should have made Rory take me to New York. I go with *you*, and end up inside a giant moose.'

Oscar walked into Madison Square Park with a sense of trepidation. He'd come here to pull off the greatest act of marksmanship since William Tell. He was going to shoot the Vykoids off the top of the heads of every NYPD Officer in the city. It was the only way he could think of to free them from their controllers.

But something felt wrong. Madison Square had emptied of troops, and Commander Strebbins was standing alone in the middle of the park. Oscar sensed a trap but, committed to the task ahead, marched solemnly forward.

He stopped ten metres away from his boss. 'Commander, I need to know if you've been compromised.'

As he spoke, his eyes scanned the ground around her feet. He could see blurs of movement and hear quiet, high-pitched chattering. She was surrounded by the Vykoids.

This time, Oscar addressed his words to them: 'I know who you are. And I will not let this happen to our great city.'

Strebbins looked interested.

Oscar continued. 'The situation has changed. This time you've given me a target. And I'm not afraid to take her down.'

He took his pistol out and aimed at Strebbins. 'If I shoot her, then this whole thing falls apart...' He felt a tap on his shoes and kicked four Vykoids away. 'I feel one more of you on me, and she dies.'

For a moment Oscar sensed the silence of the park. He felt immune from the sirens and noisy chatter of the city streets. This was just him and Strebbins.

'Put the gun down, officer. You will do as I say.'

Up until that point, Oscar had felt sure he could go through with this. But that was the voice of Jackie Strebbins, a sound he'd come to respect and fear. He told himself there was an alien under her hat, and steeled his resolve.

'This isn't you, Commander, and I am ordering you to stop.'

Commander Strebbins's face went blank for a second. Oscar guessed that the Vykoid under her hat was radioing back for advice. Oscar could see the Vykoids were moving to circle him. If he did shoot Commander Strebbins, he knew he would quickly be made into one of their puppets.

Commander Strebbins's features abruptly twisted into a contemptuous sneer. 'Go ahead and shoot,' she said.

Strebbins spread her arms out in front of her. Totally defenceless. The easiest target Oscar had ever been given.

Oscar didn't know what to do. The sight of surrender stunned him. He would need the stab of self-belief to be able to pull the trigger, and it was deserting him.

Then Strebbins took her hat off, revealing the Vykoid beneath. 'Shoot me, shoot her, take your pick,' the tiny creature shouted.

Oscar was appalled to see the tiny troll lording it over Commander Strebbins. He felt the rage building back up inside him. The Vykoid was apparently finding it so easy.

'There are hundreds of us,' the little figure taunted. 'What difference does it make if one of us dies. We'll still take your people.'

This was the extra push he needed, and Oscar began to squeeze the trigger. Then stopped. In training, Oscar had shot dozens of silhouettes and dummies. He was well practised in raising his gun to threaten or to silence. It was a way of establishing power, not doling out justice. In his time as a police officer he'd never fired a furious bullet. The anger inside him felt wrong. He was part of law *enforcement*. Not the law itself.

Commander Strebbins lifted her head, and looked Oscar in the eye. 'We took your city, without a life being lost. Now I see why!' She began to laugh.

'You're a coward. Just like the rest of your stinking, lumbering race.'

At this, Oscar tightened his grip on his gun. 'Don't say that. Stop laughing!'

But Strebbins's scorn increased. 'Look at you, all uniform and protocol and swagger. But you can't execute me. You need to see someone's back before *you* shoot. That's the problem with you big clumsy beasts. Too occupied with the small picture.'

Oscar met Strebbins's mocking gaze. The blood throbbed in his head, and his ears were ringing with adrenalin. He wanted to do the right thing. But what was it? What should he do? Whatever was on her head, Strebbins was a person and she'd done nothing wrong. She'd be an innocent casualty.

He lowered the gun, and shut his eyes, waiting for the Vykoids to come and take him.

Not content to stay at home when all the action was out on the streets, Polly had taken her class and broken in through the basement entrance of Trump Tower. They'd climbed up the service stairs, and smashed their way onto the roof. Now, lying on her belly on the roof, Polly could see the madness of the city below.

On every cross street, a line of police officers marched forwards, herding confused and scared New Yorkers in front of them. Riding on top of an armoured vehicle, Commander Strebbins broadcast to the crowds with a loudhailer, her words becoming clearer as she drew closer.

'… terrorists on the streets … bombs in the Subway … need to stay out in the open … Every building is sealed until we can be sure that the threat has passed. Until then, we ask that you remain in the open. Please give law enforcement officers your full cooperation, we will keep you informed of any developments. There are terrorists on the streets of New York…'

Polly was struck dumb by the magnitude of what was happening. How had her fellow New Yorkers become so scared of the unseen that they followed the most bizarre commands without protest? Did everyone think deep down that they *deserved* to be scared?

From so high above, the city looked like a colony of ants was being steamed out into the open. Black dots converged on Broadway from every street in New York. People seemed only too eager to follow the commands of Strebbins and her men – too focused on the unknown horror to realise what they were being asked to do.

Polly prayed for a miracle. The people she loved were being rounded up, and she couldn't do a thing to stop it. She watched as the crowds, only too happy to accept an unnamed threat, shuffled and gossiped as they marched into the Vykoid trap.

*

And across New York, every radio station, every television programme, every possible means of communication broadcast the same message:

'Follow the police to safety. The invisible menace will not defeat us! New York will not surrender! Broadway is the nominated muster station until further notice. I repeat, Broadway is the only street to have been cleared of terrorist devices.'

Chapter
21

The mammoth clambered out of the Hudson onto Liberty Island and stood dripping beside the base of the Statue of Liberty.

Sam squeezed back into the head of the mammoth. 'What now?'

'We go up, close down the Time Freeze and stop them teleporting most of Manhattan into slavery,' the Doctor replied.

'How do we do that?'

'Oh, just wait and see.'

'No, go on, tell me,' Sam asked. 'I've just swum the Hudson in an extinct animal. I think I can handle it.'

'He probably doesn't know yet,' Amy confided. 'Best not to ask.'

'Winston Churchill,' the Doctor said, to Amy's surprise. 'Winston always said he didn't want there to be a statue of him, because the pigeons would, you know, cover it in their mess. When he died, they built one anyway, and they did something extraordinary. They electrified it, so no bird would come near it.'

'Yeah? So what? We've got a city to save, don't start going all Simon Schama on me.'

'Look at this statue.' The Doctor tilted the mammoth's head back so they were staring right to the top of the Statue of Liberty. 'There's not a bird in sight. I don't think they cut the power. I think they've been using it.'

As soon as the Doctor had pointed it out, it seemed horribly obvious. Flocks of seagulls circled around the bay and turned away in the sky above Liberty Island as if they'd been shocked.

'What's it made of, Sam?' the Doctor asked.

'Steel and copper.'

'That,' said the Doctor, 'is 240 tonnes of battery. Wow, when that thing discharges, New York is going to fry.'

'What do we do?' Amy asked.

'Same as before. Only, we don't touch anything.' The Doctor smiled. 'Right, 345 steps to the top. Come on – I'll race you.'

'That sounds like a pretty lame way to make an entrance, especially to the headquarters of an alien army,' Amy commented, raising the mammoth's head again to scope out the statue. 'You know, I've got quite good on this thing…'

The Doctor broke into a huge grin. 'Go for it, Pond!'

Crashing through the ticket barriers, the monument that had welcomed so many immigrants since that first twelve million now admitted its first mammoth. Amy twisted and turned the animal on the steps. She was focused intently on her task, determined to get to the top as fast as possible.

Taking a corner too slowly, the mammoth grazed the inside of the Statue, and its fur started to smoke.

'Careful there!' the Doctor yelled.

'Thanks, Doctor,' Amy said sarcastically. 'Really helpful advice.'

At the top of the Statue, General Erik was watching their progress with disbelief. He didn't know what they were trying to achieve. Watching the crowds being squeezed onto Broadway, he dismissed the Doctor as no more than a distraction. A buzzing fly in his ear, which would soon be swatted.

With an enormous roar, the mammoth burst into the Crown Room of the Statue of Liberty, and was immediately hit with thousands of darts from the Vykoid guns.

Inside, the Doctor frantically started to hit levers.

'Doctor, it's shutting down!' Amy cried.

'I noticed…'

Out of the right eye, she could see an intrepid Vykoid scaling the mammoth's front leg. It stopped at the knee and hit a tiny button behind the kneecap.

Unexpectedly, the entire lower half of the mammoth fell to the floor and, with a heavy bump, the Doctor, Amy and Sam landed in the middle of the room, surrounded by an elite squad of Vykoid soldiers.

The Doctor was spread-eagled under the belly of the beast. He managed to pull himself out from under it, only to trip on the wet and singed mammoth fur.

'So much for an entrance,' he murmured.

General Erik strode forward. As he raised his baton, the soldiers lowered their guns.

The Doctor seemed intrigued rather than intimidated. 'Ooh, you're still moving slowly. So we're not affected by the Time Freeze in here.'

'This is a Level Five planet. How do you know about the Time Freeze?' demanded General Erik.

The Doctor grinned. 'Oh, I know lots of things, me. Not hard to work out, really. One minute you're waddling about like miniature trolls, the next you're all Wily Coyote and thinking you're the masters of the universe.'

'Correction, Doctor. The Vykoids are the race with the most refined technology of any attacking race. Now we have proven ourselves, our name shall spread throughout the galaxy and bring fear to the hearts of our enemies.'

'Nice speech! Must sound great in the War Rooms on Vykoid. Brilliant minds, but you guys miss the point sometimes. Like the reach of that second-hand teleport beam is only, what, thirty metres? You'd need to be very lucky to get what you want with that…'

'Or very clever.'

'True, that's also true. But I've noticed you keep waving that baton around like it's the answer to everything, and I think I know why.'

The Doctor grabbed at General Erik's hand and came away with the tiny baton. It was barely a centimetre long and covered with alien symbols.

'Reactions are a bit slow there, Erik. You've been relying on this Time Freeze thing for too long, you've got slack.'

'What is it, Doctor?' Amy asked.

'It's a remote control. Oh you are such a bloke, Erik, you just have to keep it where no one else can change the channel. Honestly, look at you here, hanging out with all your boys, polishing each other's armour all day long, waiting for the day you get to dominate another city. Still, no one gets to do much if I can do this…'

The Doctor took a needle out of his pocket and jabbed at three points on the baton. The vortex of green light changed to orange, and a huge wave rolled out across Manhattan.

'Now that's better. Isn't that clever? Unless your little people jockeys have got a bit faster, the police won't be moving quite as niftily any more. That's the problem with relying on modern technology, you see. Me, I just have a good old sonic— Oh.'

General Erik was grinning. He looked like an expert poker player who had picked too ignorant an opponent, and was disappointed by his lack of effort. 'Move, and I'll shoot her,' he said.

Sam Horwitz was holding a gun to Amy's head and was forcing her down onto the floor.

'No, Sam!' The Doctor was horrified.

As he held her tight, Amy could see that a tiny Vykoid had dug a control chair through Sam's messy hair and was gleefully controlling him. Sam had become a puppet of the Vykoid Army.

Amy kicked and struggled, her elbows digging into Sam as she tried to fight him off. But Sam overpowered Amy and pinned her to the floor.

General Erik strolled over and regarded Amy at her eye level.

'Oi, troll-face!' Amy yelled at him. 'Tell him to let go of me.'

General Erik ignored her. 'Fascinating… You're so important to him, and you don't know why.'

'You better let go of me, or he's going to do something terrible to you…'

If General Erik was at all moved by Amy's big, fierce eyes, he didn't show it. Instead, he called his lieutenant forward and instructed him to kill Amy Pond.

On top of Trump Tower, Joe turned to Polly and asked: 'Will my dad be OK?'

Polly didn't know what to say.

Millie pulled at her hand. 'Shouldn't the Doctor be doing something now?'

Again, Polly was stumped. Far below, she could see that people were beginning to panic. The police were shoving the crowds along, truncheons drawn as they ordered everyone to cram onto Broadway. Polly could imagine how terrified they must feel down there. Squad cars were lining up on each cross street, lights flashing and sirens blaring. They had shut the city down, and no one knew why.

Chapter
22

Inside the Statue of Liberty, the Doctor and Amy had their hands tied and were taken from the Crown Room. As Sam dragged them out, Amy could see General Erik take his position at the window, ready to start transporting the people of New York to the asteroid mines.

As soon as they were out of earshot, Amy started on the Doctor.

'Why did you surrender?'

'They were going to kill you!'

'But you gave him back that remote control thing. There are millions of people out there!'

'Did I mention, he was going to shoot you?'

'I thought you'd do something clever.'

'Yeah, me saving you, that was the clever bit.

Honestly, Amy, is being brave not good enough for you? I thought you'd be showering me in kisses.'

Amy snorted. 'Unlikely. Not if it means I'll be mining fossilised Space-Boar droppings for the rest of my life.'

The Doctor sighed.

Amy hadn't finished yet. 'So what are you going to do?'

'Where do you think we are, Amy?'

'I don't know. Some kind of round hut thing? Oh, don't go changing the subject on me.'

But the Doctor was too interested in his surroundings. They had been tied up and dumped inside the Torch of the Statue of Liberty.

Sam Horwitz stood back, and looked at them with a disinterested expression. 'You'll be pleased to know that you've been chosen as the first. It is a great honour. The General himself has overturned your evaluations to ensure you have a long and glorious service in the mines.'

'Sam – can you bend down?' Amy whispered. 'I want to tell you something.'

Sam obliged. And Amy headbutted him hard on the side of the head. The controlling Vykoid clung on for his life, digging his hands into Sam's hair. But he hadn't been dislodged, and Sam stepped back.

The Vykoid was laughing at Amy now. 'Did you ever look at big animals and wonder why they were so stupid?'

Amy stamped her foot in frustration. 'Yeah, I get it. But I'm not the one drowning in dandruff and hair gel.'

'Sam.' The Doctor looked deadly serious. 'Sam, I need you to listen very carefully. Somewhere in there, Sam is still alive. You are more than a puppet, and you need to try very hard to remember that.'

The Vykoid controlling Sam laughed hysterically. 'Why are you even trying? It's like cattle going to the market. You are going to be sold, so stop mooing.'

The Doctor wasn't put off. 'Sam, you need to listen to me. This city was built on dreams of freedom. The American dream wasn't built on might and weapons. It was built by hard work and the hope of freedom on the other side. That's why you came here, that's why your great grandparents came here. This is the city of the free, and no one in it, simply no one, can ever accept being a slave. Focus on that feeling, Sam, the dream of freedom you have in you – use it to overpower what you're feeling.'

Amy leant close to the Doctor and whispered, 'Do you think it'll work?'

The Doctor met Sam's eyes and continued. 'You need to believe in yourself, Sam. You are more than this, you are not meant to be a slave. Sam – this is your big day. The moment you become famous. Help me, and I can stop this happening. Trust me, Sam, and trust yourself.'

The Vykoid controller looked rattled. He pulled

on the levers, but it seemed that Sam was no longer responding. Moving so fast he was a blur of energy, the controller was slamming buttons and yanking every control he had, but to no avail.

With every movement an obvious effort, Sam raised his hand, grasped the Vykoid and yanked the chair from his head. 'Ow!' he winced as the tiny wires they'd drilled into his skull ripped out. He bent double, but then straightened up with pride.

'I did it!'

The Vykoid was dangling from Sam's hand, furiously trying to bite and scratch his way free.

'As for you...' Sam lifted the Vykoid higher. 'How dare you do this to me?' He inspected the troll-like figure with a scientist's eye. 'What an ugly little creature you are.'

'Over here, Sam.' The Doctor was holding out his hand. Carefully taking the Vykoid by the scruff of the neck, he took out the sonic screwdriver and scanned the small creature from head to toe. 'Here, hold this. Gentle with him now.'

The Doctor handed the Vykoid to Amy and clambered up to the top of the Torch. Standing precariously on the crossbeams, he touched the sonic screwdriver to the very peak of the Torch and then leapt down, a huge grin on his face.

'Done!'

'Is that it?' Amy said, bewildered. 'Here, take this back... I don't want him.'

The Vykoid's leathery face was screwed up and knotted with anger.

'Ah, let him go,' said the Doctor. 'He can't stop us now.'

Amy dropped the Vykoid to the floor and dusted her hands together, glad to be rid of the alien. 'So why are you looking so pleased with yourself?' she asked.

The Doctor led Amy and Sam to a tiny porthole and looked out towards New York.

'That's one of the biggest cities in the world,' he told them. 'The best of everything is there. But it's not about being bigger. It doesn't matter who has the biggest guns or the most money or the most troops. The mightiest army can fall to the smallest. The Vykoids showed us that. But they made a mistake, a tiny mistake. They should have killed us when they had the chance.'

'What have you done?' Sam asked.

'I can't make the mob turn on them. I can't even stop the Time Freeze. But I can do something they don't expect…'

'Which is?'

'That teleport beam. They've programmed it for humans.'

'Yeah, I gathered,' Amy said.

'Erik does everything with his remote control. Very technological race, the Vykoids, they love to put too many functions into a device. Their beam comes from the highest point of the Statue of Liberty.' The Doctor pointed up. 'Right here.'

Amy looked out. 'But they're all still captives. The Vykoids have rounded everyone up.'

The Doctor grinned. 'That teleport beam is going to leave the people of New York exactly where they are. But the police officers might lose something on their heads…'

In the Crown Room, General Erik checked his watch and nodded to his men. He picked up his radio, and issued the command. 'We are good to go. I'd like to thank the puppeteers for their sterling work.'

Around him, the Vykoids scurried around a control room, and the green vortex grew in intensity like a mini-star. It burnt so brightly that the entire top half of the Statue of Liberty became luminescent.

Holding his baton in front of him as if it were the key to life itself, General Erik pressed a button. A vast beam leapt out of the vortex, sprang to the Torch on the top of the Statue of Liberty and arced through the air towards Broadway. As it touched the ground, it crackled and smoked. The ground shook, and smoke rose from the tarmac.

The beam idled for a moment on the south of Manhattan. Then, with a flick of General Erik's wrist, it snaked and turned along the jagged line of Broadway, leaving a cloud of smoke in its wake. As it reached the top of the island, General Erik turned the beam off with a triumphant wave of his hand.

'It is done. Ten seconds – that's all it took!' General Erik pushed his sense of dignity to one side and did a little dance on the windowsill. 'We have taken New York. If I can make it here, I'll make it anywhere!'

General Erik was already dreaming of the rewards he would have lavished on him in the Vykoid halls. They'd build a statue of him twice the size of the Statue of Liberty. It would be the Statue of Victory, and it would bear his name.

He picked up his radio and called Commander Strebbins. 'Lars! Come in. I am ready to hear your report.'

There was no reply, but General Erik wasn't daunted.

'Stop celebrating, you hothead! We have another five transports to do before the day is done.'

Again there was no reply. General Erik flicked a switch on his radio and tried again.

'Red? Are you receiving? Red?'

Another Vykoid clambered up and whispered in his general's ear.

With a mounting sense of dread, General Erik took the telescope that the private thrust into his hand, and gazed out at Manhattan.

The people of Manhattan were still crammed into Broadway. But on every street, the NYPD officers were scratching their heads and wondering what on earth was going on. Their Vykoid controllers had gone. Teleported back to their home planet.

For a whole minute General Erik said nothing.

The Doctor stood in the doorway.

General Erik faced him with tiny tears falling from his red eyes onto his wrinkled face, and he howled. He felt like a mouse caught in a trap, and took little satisfaction from the sight of the Doctor recoiling from the noise of his painful and ugly rage.

'You have tricked me, Doctor.'

The Doctor walked forward, and crouched down to General Erik's level. 'I'm sorry, Erik, I really am, but I couldn't let you do it.'

'But we are better than them. They are only oafs. We are the true race.'

'That's where you are very wrong. They may be stupid and clumsy and selfish, but they are the most brilliant people you will ever meet. Right now, there are men and women who deserve to live freely, with no one telling them what to do, and without fear that someone might tear their city to pieces overnight. And as long as you keep on thinking that they deserve less, I will keep on stopping you.'

If General Erik had grown conceited with success, he now seemed puzzled by the humility of failure. 'How can I return empty-handed?'

He realised instantly that the question had been

a mistake. There was a hint of anger in the Doctor's crooked smile, and General Erik found himself backing away.

The Doctor spoke quietly. 'You should count yourself lucky. You fought and lost, and will go home as free men. We've been kinder to you than you've been to *any* planet you've conquered. And when you get back, tell everyone you meet that this planet is not prepared to be enslaved. Tell them they have a great champion and a great warrior.'

The Doctor bent down towards General Erik and whispered in his ear. Two words.

'You better go before the boat tours start.'

The Doctor, Amy and Sam were standing on Liberty Island with the mammoth. General Erik was at their feet, gazing over the city he'd failed to conquer.

The Doctor held out his hand and General Erik handed him the baton. 'It's time you left, Erik.'

The Vykoid General stood in front of his most senior officers, thanking them one by one. It was obvious to Amy that they meant nothing to him. He had no affection or gratitude for any of them.

'Oh, er, sorry about the insides,' Amy said, nodding at the mammoth. 'We had to make some room.'

General Erik saluted farewell and joined the columns of Vykoid soldiers retreating onto the belly of the mammoth. With a gentle tick of clockwork, the army was lifted back inside the mammoth. It shut with a quiet clunk and, moments later, an eerie green light blasted out, filling the air with that strange high-pitched screech. The sphere of green boiling light engulfed the mammoth and spread out, pulsing as if ready to explode over the city.

But this time it snapped inwards, and a crash rang out, echoing like a thousand cymbals tumbling to the floor.

The mammoth was gone.

Amy gave the Doctor a massive hug. 'Now tell me what you did.'

'Simple really. I changed the genetic profile of the teleport beam. Took a scan from the Vykoid controlling Sam, fed it into the teleport transmitter, and it took all the Vykoids back home. Smallest thing we did today.'

Sam stepped forward. 'If you don't mind, Doctor, I have a question. All you said, about freedom and dreams, is it true?'

'Worked on you, didn't it? Have you heard the story about the richest man in America? He arrived in New York with nothing but two potatoes, he sold those and bought four potatoes, sold them and bought eight potatoes, in ten years time he was selling potatoes up and down the East Coast. Pretty soon he was so rich he had people to chew his own chips for him.'

'Really?' Sam said excitedly. 'Do you think that's how it works? Could it happen to anyone?'

'To you? Oh no, you'd make a terrible potato dealer. You're far better than that. You brought an alien army to New York, and then sent them back again. That's as good as it gets.'

Chapter

23

The Doctor stood in Times Square and clicked his fingers. The TARDIS faded into view.

There was no sign that the mammoth had ever existed. The streets had been cleared of debris, and the road works and building sites of New York were back in action, churning out dust and noise. Nobody would ever know they had all been seconds away from working for the Vykoids.

'Stop, police!'

The Doctor looked around him.

'It's Oscar,' Amy told him. 'Hi, Oscar.'

Oscar looked at the Doctor and Amy, as if he was struggling to remember them. 'How do you know my name?'

Amy grinned. 'Lucky guess.'

'Right.' Oscar frowned. 'Well, you can't leave this box here.'

'We're not going to,' the Doctor said.

'And, Oscar,' Amy said, 'you've been brilliant.'

The Doctor and Amy stepped back inside the TARDIS, and Oscar stared after them in wonder.

'Why didn't he know who we were?' Amy asked.

'I think the Time Freeze is going to have a terrible effect on their short-term memories. When their brains sped up again, they lost a lot of what happened, maybe all of it. They'll never know.'

Amy strolled over to the Doctor, who was leaning back on the console, 'So that's it? You saved the world, and nobody ever knows?'

'*We* saved the world, Amy. People will forget, but we know that we got rid of the Forgotten Army of the Vykoids. Never let anyone take that away from you.' The Doctor paused. 'Although you will, like the Vykoids, be forgotten. Still, *I'll* always know, and that's what counts. Amy Pond, there's a name – you could be a queen in a fairy tale.' The Doctor rolled the words around, speaking them grandly to the corners of the TARDIS: 'The mighty Amelia Pond, Saviour of New York!'

'Yeah, shut up,' Amy mumbled. She wasn't used to receiving compliments that she hadn't demanded.

The Doctor just laughed.

Amy looked at the Doctor with interest. 'How come you find it so easy to leave? Don't you ever wonder what happened to everyone – Sam and Polly, and Oscar, and poor old Commander Strebbins.'

The Doctor skidded round the glass floor of the TARDIS. 'Nah, they'll be fine... Although I never got to show you the bar where the Governor of New Amsterdam lost the city in a bet. Bad day, I was busy on the Bronx peace talks. Well, they say they were talks, felt more like a barn dance to me. I thought I told you to stop me if I rambled?'

Amy laughed at her Doctor, still raggedy in so many ways. 'I've given up trying. You *never* stop talking!'

'You love it really.'

The Doctor ignored the face Amy was pulling, and pulled four levers in different directions. The vworp of the TARDIS engines began, and the bubbles of blown glass started to groan up and down in the console.

'Next stop,' the Doctor announced, 'the Delirium Archive. There are Magnatine Dynasty crystals so beautiful they'll make your hair go curly with delight. Or maybe with boredom... Anyway, we'll find out soon!'

On the New York street outside, Mr Germowski was surprised to see the shiny blue box parked on the pavement fade and disappear with a loud rasping, groaning sound. Still, at least he had his pitch back. He wheeled his pretzel stall into position, and hollered into the street.

'Pretzels three dollars!'

To his surprise, the weird noise returned, and the blue box shuddered back into view. It was almost as if they'd heard his shouting.

A young man with floppy hair leaned out of the blue box, with a big grin on his long face. He gave the stunned Germowski a ten dollar bill, and took three pretzels.

'Do you know, one of these saved New York earlier today?' the man said cheerfully.

Germowski was gobsmacked, and could only stare as, with a cheery wave, the man shut the door and the blue box once more faded away.

* * *

Far away from Earth, a tiny Vykoid stood in a vast hall, spiky helmet in hand, facing the Committee for Unsuccessful Invasions. It was time for him to explain why he had returned from Earth empty-handed. And General Erik had only one answer to give. Two words:

'Amy Pond.'

The inside scoop on 900 years of travel aboard the Doctor's famous time machine.

Everything you need to know about the TARDIS is here – where it came from, where it's been, how it works, and how it has changed since we first encountered it in that East London junkyard in 1963.

Including photographs, design drawings and concept artwork from different eras of the series, this handbook explores the ship's endless interior, looking inside its wardrobe and bedrooms, its power rooms and sick bay, its corridors and cloisters, and revealing just how the show's production teams have created the dimensionally transcendental police box, inside and out.

The TARDIS Handbook is the essential guide to the best ship in the universe.

Coming soon from BBC Books:

DOCTOR WHO
Nuclear Time
by Oli Smith

£6.99 ISBN 978 1 846 07989 4

Colorado, 1981. The Doctor, Amy and Rory arrive in Appletown – an idyllic village in the remote American desert where the townsfolk go peacefully about their suburban routines. But when two more strangers arrive, things begin to change.

The first is a mad scientist – whose warnings are cut short by an untimely and brutal death. The second is the Doctor…

As death falls from the sky, the Doctor is trapped. The TARDIS is damaged, and the Doctor finds he is living backwards through time. With Amy and Rory being hunted through the suburban streets of the Doctor's own future and getting farther away with every passing second, he must unravel the secrets of Appletown before time runs out…

A thrilling, all-new adventure featuring the Doctor, Amy and Rory, as played by Matt Smith, Karen Gillan and Arthur Darvill in the spectacular hit series from BBC Television.

An archaeological dig in 1936 unearths relics of another time… And – as the Doctor, Amy and Rory realise – another place. Another planet.

But if Enola Porter, noted adventuress, has really found evidence of an alien civilisation, how come she isn't famous? Why has Rory never heard of her? Added to that, since Amy's been travelling with him for a while now, why does she now think the Doctor is from Mars?

As the ancient spaceship reactivates, the Doctor discovers that nothing and no one can be trusted. The things that seem most real could actually be literal fabrications – and very deadly indeed.

Who can the Doctor believe when no one is what they seem? And how can he defeat an enemy who can bend matter itself to their will? For the Doctor, Amy and Rory – and all of humanity – the buried secrets of the past are very much a threat to the present…

A thrilling, all-new adventure featuring the Doctor, Amy and Rory, as played by Matt Smith, Karen Gillan and Arthur Darvill in the spectacular hit series from BBC Television.

DOCTOR◉WHO
The Only Good Dalek

by Justin Richards and Mike Collins

£16.99 ISBN 978 1 846 07984 9

Station 7 is where the Earth Forces send all the equipment captured in their unceasing war against the Daleks. It's where Dalek technology is analysed and examined. It's where the Doctor and Amy have just arrived. But somehow the Daleks have found out about Station 7 – and there's something there that they want back.

With the Doctor increasingly worried about the direction the Station's research is taking, the commander of Station 7 knows he has only one possible, desperate, defence. Because the last terrible secret of Station 7 is that they don't only store captured Dalek technology. It's also a prison. And the only thing that might stop a Dalek is another Dalek…

An epic, full-colour graphic novel featuring the Doctor and Amy, as played by Matt Smith and Karen Gillan in the spectacular hit series from BBC Television.